The Brothers of the Sled

by
John H. Leeper

 AMBASSADOR

 EMERALD

The Brothers of the Sled

Copyright © 1996 John Leeper

This edition 1996

All Scripture quotations are from the King James Version.

ISBN 1 889893 01 3

Published by

EMERALD HOUSE GROUP, INC.

1 Chick Springs Road, Suite 206
Greenville, South Carolina 29609

AMBASSADOR PRODUCTIONS, LTD.

Providence House
16 Hillview Avenue,
Belfast, BT5 6JR

For my daughter,
Rachele Erika Xenos Leeper

Contents

The Brothers of the Sled

PART 1: THE MAN'S CAMP

Kam-Yuk was born one spring, long ago, to the world of man and the Yukon Territory. His parents were sled dogs like their parents and grandparents before them. So when he was very young, shuffling around the pens built for the puppies and their mothers, nothing seemed more natural to him than the thought that one day he would grow up and wear a leather harness and traces and pull the man's sled across the ice and snow.

In fact, Kam-Yuk looked forward to that day as he did no other. The strange sights and sounds and smells of the man's camp were wonderful to him. Some mornings, the air was charged with excitement. Sled dogs ran this way and that between the man's log cabin, barns, and animal pens. A few carried large bundles slung across their backs. Others pulled loads that were lashed between two long sticks and strapped to their sides. Still others were joined into a team to drag the man's long wooden sled. Then the man led them into the mountains

and forests surrounding the camp. Often they would be gone for a very long time. To Kam-Yuk it seemed mysterious and full of the promise of adventure.

He knew that every adult dog in the camp, small or great, male or female, had sworn loyalty, love, and life to the man. They called themselves "the Brothers of the Sled," and whatever the man asked of them they did without so much as a growl or whimper. Their leader was named Uther. He was a large gray and black husky with bright, piercing blue eyes. Kam-Yuk often saw him at night, trotting about the camp, making sure that all was safe and secure. Now and then, Uther would stop near the puppy pens, raise his muzzle to the stars, and sing of the Brotherhood. When he did, the voices of the other sled dogs quickly joined his.

"We are the Brothers of the Sled;
    By the powerful hand of the man we are led.
No snow too deep, no path too long,
    No weight too heavy to silence our song.
Shoulder to shoulder and heel to toe,
    Hunger and fear we never shall know.
Dogs of one heart may it always be said;
    For we are the Brothers, the Brothers, the
Brothers . . . Oh, we are the Brothers of the Sled!"

Some nights the singing lasted many hours, for there were more verses to the song than Kam-Yuk could count. They spoke of sled dog heroes and great deeds of daring performed for the man. On nights like these, Kam-Yuk often fell asleep with the music of the sled dog choir drumming softly in his ears. He would curl himself into a little ball of fur alongside his mother and dream of a time when he would run before a powerful team of huskies,

9

breaking a trail through the snow for the man's sled. He would be a great leader like Uther. Even greater! One day young dogs would sing of his deeds.

But Kam-Yuk was very young then, and he knew nothing of the wilderness around the mountain camp or of the creatures who roamed its vast expanse.

The first real surprise in Kam-Yuk's life came when he learned there were dogs in the Yukon that did not pull sleds. One snowy night during his first Yukon winter, a stranger was brought into camp by the man. One end of a long rope was looped around the dog's neck. The other end was held firmly by the man, who stood on the runners at the rear of Uther's sled. At times, the stranger jogged quietly along behind the sled. But now and then he fought the rope savagely and was dragged through the snow.

By this time Kam-Yuk was old enough to wander free about the camp. He was locked in a pen only at night with his mother, brothers, and sisters. So when morning came and he was free to roam, he had a chance to study this new dog closely. The animal was very strange. He was long-legged and ugly. His gray fur was thick and shaggy. His face and sides carried the scars of old, deep wounds. Kam-Yuk heard the other huskies say that the newcomer was more wolf than dog; and even though he had never seen a wolf, he knew from the look of the stranger that it had to be a terrifying beast.

But for some reason the man seemed to take a keen interest in this stranger. He treated the new dog with great kindness and patience and even gave him portions of food from his own table. Often the man would go to the newcomer's pen and stand there for hours at a time talking quietly to him. This made Uther and the other

10

huskies trust the stranger. They quickly grew to ignore his differences and helped him adjust to life in the man's camp. In no time at all, it seemed, he was broken to harness and became a trusted member of the sled team.

But Kam-Yuk could never get used to the sound and look and smell of this animal from the wilderness. And to make matters worse, Half-Wolf, as Uther and the other huskies called the stranger, made a point of seeking out every young dog in camp and telling them stories of his life in the wild. They were dark, terrible tales full of pain, fear, loneliness, and death. And they so terrified Kam-Yuk that whenever he saw Half-Wolf coming, he would run away and hide in his pen to keep from hearing them.

For the longest time after Kam-Yuk heard the horrible stories of Half-Wolf, he wondered why any dog would want to live in the wilderness away from the safety of the man's camp. But then he met the second wild dog.

It was early in the spring, shortly after Kam-Yuk's first birthday. The stranger crept into camp one evening on his own and prowled silently around the man's cabin picking up scraps of food. He held his head low as though fearing attack. Uther and the other huskies tried to make him welcome, but for some reason he did not get along well with anyone. He was quick to start a quarrel, and if any of the man's dogs came too close he would run away from them, snarling angrily.

But to Kam-Yuk this stranger was neither as ugly nor as frightening as Half-Wolf. So that night, when the wild dog wandered near his pen, Kam-Yuk stopped him and asked about the wilderness. The stories this dog told were not at all like the terrible tales of Half-Wolf. In fact they made the rugged mountains, dark forests, and deep

11

valleys sound very beautiful and exciting. He spoke of a pack of wild dogs, much greater in number than the Brotherhood, that lived and hunted around the man's camp—dogs who had never once been locked in a pen or tied to a sled. Kam-Yuk was thrilled by the tales the stranger told him. But suddenly his mother woke up, saw the wild dog standing outside the pen, and warned him away from her son.

Next morning the newcomer was gone. The young sled dog asked his mother if he would return. But she shook her head and replied, "His heart is wild. He could not be one of us." All of this made Kam-Yuk very curious about the wilderness and the strange dogs who lived there.

Kam-Yuk's life might have continued from that day with no more surprises. He could have grown up to be exactly like the other huskies in the camp, and his curiosity about the wilderness might have slowly disappeared. But that was not to be. Three events were to change his entire life and send him along a different trail from the one chosen by his mother, brothers, and sisters.

Late in the summer, when the weather was hot and there was little for the huskies to do, but plod around the dusty camp and look for cool places to nap, Kam-Yuk's father suddenly grew ill. His father was a small gray husky named Roc. He was not a great leader like Uther. But he was a loyal sled dog and obedient, and he pulled his weight in the team. All the huskies in camp were his friends.

Roc was given a bed of soft blankets in a shed where the older sled dogs lived and plenty of food and water. Every day Kam-Yuk and his mother went to visit him.

12

For hours at a time they would sit beside him, watching him sleep. Kam-Yuk lost any desire to play with the other pups in the camp. All he wanted to do was sit beside his father in the dark shed and dream of the day when Roc would again be well and take his place in the sled team.

Often the other huskies came and sat with him as well. Most believed the man would heal him. Their visits made Roc more cheerful.

But as the days passed, Kam-Yuk noticed that his father was sleeping more and more and eating very little. He became terribly worried. Sometimes he would go to the man's cabin and stand outside the door, whimpering for him to come and heal his father. But the man never seemed to hear him.

Then one morning when Kam-Yuk awoke and went to the shed where Roc was kept, he found Uther waiting for him. Uther blocked his path and shook his huge head from side to side. "Your father is gone, Kam-Yuk," he said softly. "His work in the camp ended last night, and the man carried him away. Your mother and I were with him at the end. He suffered no pain, and he was happy."

Kam-Yuk howled in dismay. Uther stepped toward him and said, "Roc was a mighty sled dog. His death is a great loss to the Brotherhood. But he was very proud of you. Of all his sons and daughters, you were the one he hoped would one day take his place in the team."

Something in Uther's words and voice caused Kam-Yuk to stop howling. But it did not ease his sorrow.

That night the Brothers of the Sled sang for many hours. Their stories spoke of his father's courage and greatness. Kam-Yuk's mother sang with them. But the young sled dog did not. For the first time in his life, nothing in the songs of the Brotherhood stirred his heart.

13

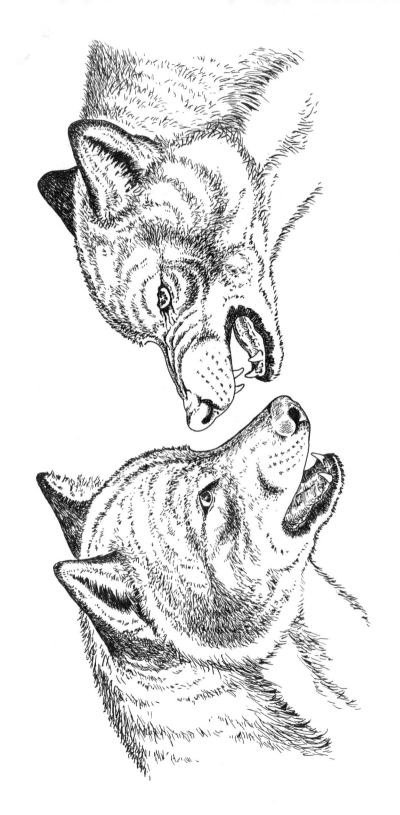

All that he felt was a great emptiness inside and anger at the man, who had been unable or unwilling to save his father's life.

A few weeks later came the second event in Kam-Yuk's life that was to turn him against the man.

In the days that followed his father's death, Kam-Yuk grew very close to Uther. The great leader of the Brotherhood had always been his hero. And Uther noticed the deep sadness in this young husky and wanted to help. So he singled Kam-Yuk out from the other young dogs for special attention.

Uther's kindness helped fill the emptiness in Kam-Yuk's heart. And in turn, his loyalty and devotion to Uther grew with each passing day.

One afternoon in the fall, when all of the huskies in the man's camp were busy preparing for the winter's work ahead, something unexpected happened. Kam-Yuk saw Uther and Half-Wolf meet at the center of the camp. An argument began. In the beginning, it was no more than a growl. But soon there were snarling and snapping. Then a terrible fight began. Uther and Half-Wolf lunged at each other. Their fangs clashed savagely. They hammered one another with their heavy shoulders as each tried to throw the other to the ground.

The fight spread quickly among the other dogs in the camp. From the day he had arrived, Half Wolf had proved by his strength and courage that he was a mighty sled dog. Many believed he should now be leader of the Brotherhood instead of Uther. The battle was so terrible that some huskies would have been badly injured or even killed had the man not rushed from his cabin with whip and club to stop them.

Kam-Yuk was certain the man would punish Half-Wolf

for challenging Uther. But no! He delivered as many blows to the one as he did the other. Soon the warring pair cringed at his feet, and all fighting stopped. Then, instead of forcing Half-Wolf to take his place in the team, the man separated him and his followers from the dogs loyal to Uther. He dragged a new sled from his barn and made it clear to every husky in camp that Half-Wolf and his dogs were to pull it.

Kam-Yuk stared after the man in bitter silence. First he had allowed Roc to die, and now he was being unfair to Uther, who had served him loyally for so many years.

That night Kam-Yuk was too restless to sleep. While his mother, brothers, and sisters huddled together inside their hutch, the young husky paced angrily up and down the length of the pen. He thought hard about everything he had seen that day and wondered what he should do.

Then a strange sound reached his ears. It drifted into the camp on the night wind. Kam-Yuk went to the fence and thrust his head between the slats of wood. There on a hill high above the man's camp stood the most beautiful dog he had ever seen in his life. Her coat was pure white and shone in the moonlight. Her body was lean and strong. She raised her muzzle and sang a song that had no melody or rhyme.

"Dogs to leather harness and whips were not born;
But to the freedom of forest, mountain, and wind.
In the wild a dog finds true meat. Elk and deer.
Not the tasteless food of man.
Why serve pain and sorrow
When freedom and life are so near?
Dogs of man are not brothers,
But enemies of each other and of wind, mountain, and forest.
Dogs to leather harness and whips were not born."

16

When the beautiful white dog finished
turned suddenly and vanished into the for
felt a strange thrill at the sound of her voic
to hear more and started to call out to her
recalled how angry his mother had been w..... sne saw
the second wild dog near their pen. So he stood there in
silence thinking about the words the dog sang. He
remembered his father's death and the fight between
Uther and Half-Wolf. And for the first time in his life, he
thought of the dried fish and meal the man fed him. His
mouth and stomach longed for something better, but
exactly what he was not certain. Then he faced the man's
cabin and to his surprise, heard himself growling.

Late the next night the white dog returned, and this
time she gave her name—Varya! Kam-Yuk thought it
was the most beautiful name he had ever heard. He
listened hard to her strange sounding music. He did not
want to miss a single word. Varya told him of the freedom
he could have if only he would come to run and hunt
with her in the wilderness. She called the man cruel for
chaining dogs to a life they were never meant to live.
She said the man's camp was just a tiny clearing in the
middle of a huge, wonderful world. And the verses of
her song told of dogs who lived in the wild and were
much greater than Uther.

Suddenly Kam-Yuk spotted Half-Wolf. He appeared
from the shadows around the man's cabin and began
trotting out of the camp in Varya's direction with his
head low, growling angrily. She quickly vanished. This
made Kam-Yuk hate Half-Wolf even more. He so loved
the sound of Varya's voice that he wanted to hear her
music all night long.

Varya did not return to the hill above the man's camp

17

any weeks. Still, no matter how cold the night might come, Kam-Yuk would sit for hours in one corner of his pen, peering through a crack in the boards, watching hopefully for her. He thought there was nothing so beautiful in the whole world as the white Varya. And as he sat alone thinking about her song, he began to change—not in face or body but deep in his heart. The change was so gradual that at first Kam-Yuk himself did not notice it.

Varya sounded so wonderfully wise and she looked so perfect that the huskies in the man's camp seemed stupid and ugly alongside her. Even Uther lost his place as a hero to Kam-Yuk. Once the sounds and smells and sights of the camp excited him, but now they only bothered him or made him angry or sick to his stomach.

The fall was short that year. The first blizzard of the winter swept over the mountains from the northwest and covered the Yukon with a blanket of white. As soon as the storm cleared, the man came for Kam-Yuk. The young husky was now big enough to be broken to the sled. So he put a rope around Kam-Yuk's neck and led him to a place where two dogs waited for them. These huskies were much too old to pull a heavy load, so the man only used them to train his young dogs. Kam-Yuk was fastened into a harness between the pair, and the traces were hitched to a small sled.

When Kam-Yuk was a puppy, he thought this would be the happiest day of his life. He would learn the way of the harness, serve the man, and become a Brother of the Sled. Instead, this day turned out to be the blackest. The harness collar was heavy and rubbed his shoulders raw. The two old dogs were very strict with him, especially the leader. Whenever he got out of line, the

18

lead dog would spin around and nip him on the nose or side.

Then there was the weight of the sled itself. Even though it was small and held no cargo, Kam-Yuk thought they might as well be towing the man's log cabin. He was exhausted in five minutes. But whenever he slowed to rest, the old dog behind him snapped at his heels and ordered him to pull harder. Worst of all was the man's whip. Twice, Kam-Yuk tangled the traces and heard it crack in the air. Both times its leather strap stung his back.

Kam-Yuk pulled the training sled for only an hour, but he felt as though he had worked the entire day. When he was taken back to his pen, he was so tired that he fell asleep instantly and did not awaken until he heard Varya's voice calling to him on the night wind.

Kam-Yuk sprang to his feet. He was stiff and sore, but a wild rage burned inside him and gave him new strength. He hated the man and his whip. He hated the sled dogs and their stupid fights. But most of all he hated the harness and the sled, which he blamed for killing his father. He would be free of this terrible place!

There was a weak plank in the fence of his pen. Kam Yuk found it and with his teeth and shoulders he tore and shoved with all his might. Wood cracked. Nails groaned. Then the plank fell, leaving an opening just wide enough for Kam-Yuk to squeeze through.

Across the snow he ran as fast as he could. He ran toward the sound of Varya's beautiful voice deep in the wilderness. And he swore to himself that the man's camp was behind him forever.

PART 2: THE WILDERNESS

Varya's song drew Kam-Yuk deeper and deeper into the forest. Every time he reached a spot where he thought she was waiting for him, he discovered that her voice was coming from beyond another ridge.

Each step carried the young husky higher into the rugged Yukon mountains. He ran for hours. Not once did he stop to rest as he climbed the steep trails. His hatred of the man's camp drove him forward. But when the sun finally broke above the cliffs in the east, the strength in Kam-Yuk's legs left him. He fell panting into the snow at the edge of an open meadow.

Kam-Yuk listened hard for Varya's song, but all he could hear was the whisper of the wind in the tops of the pine trees. He turned his head to see how far he had traveled in the night. Below him, spread out for miles in every direction, where green fir trees and fields of snow. Only a thin white line rising from the foot of the eastern mountains showed him the location of the man's camp. He knew it was smoke from the chimney of the log cabin.

As tired as he was, Kam-Yuk felt light-hearted and happy. Every verse of Varya's song seemed true. The man's camp was just a tiny clearing in the middle of a huge, beautiful world. Now he was free of that terrible little place. He was free of the dog pens and the sleds and the whip of the man. He was free to run and hunt with Varya in the wild.

Suddenly Kam-Yuk heard a deep-throated growl behind him. He jumped to his feet and spun around only to find that he was nose to nose with a huge, gray dog. The animal was thin and shaggy. Kam-Yuk thought he might be a brother to Half-Wolf.

Before the young husky could speak, the gray dog raised his nose toward the sky and gave a terrible howl. Wild dogs came running toward them from every direction. In seconds, Kam-Yuk was surrounded by a snarling pack.

He cowered in the snow, and one of the wild dogs growled, "Where did he come from?"

Said another, "He smells like the man's camp!"

"Then we should kill him!" cried a third. "There is no room for anything that smells of man among us!"

To Kam-Yuk's horror, there was a rumble of agreement from the throats of the other dogs. The pack formed a tight circle around him and closed in. Long, white fangs gleamed savagely from all sides.

"Stop!" came a loud bark. Instantly the line of wild dogs parted. Into the middle of the circle trotted the biggest dog Kam-Yuk had ever seen. He was jet black from nose to tail. He had thick, shiny hair, a wide chest, and long, powerful legs. At his heels walked Varya.

Immediately, Kam-Yuk sprang to his feet and pranced toward her. But the black dog lunged at him, struck him with a shoulder, and knocked him back into the snow. "Not so fast!" he growled. "Who are you, and how did you get here?"

"My name is Kam-Yuk," the young husky

whimpered. "I escaped last night from the man's camp."

Kam-Yuk could not take his eyes off Varya. Before this, he had only been able to admire her at a great distance. But now they were finally together, and her beauty seemed a thousand times greater. Suddenly the young husky forgot his fear and barked to her lovingly. "You are the most beautiful dog in the world. I heard your voice calling me, and I followed you all night. I would follow you anywhere! I want to be with you for the rest of my life!"

The wild dogs around him began to howl with laughter. And Varya shouted, "One thing is for certain; this pup has good eyes," which made them laugh even louder.

Finally the black dog called for quiet. He grinned at Kam-Yuk and said, "Pup, I am afraid you have much to learn. You might have followed Varya's voice into the wilderness, but from this moment on you must follow mine if you want to stay. You see, I am Sagun, leader of the pack. Varya is my mate!"

Kam-Yuk stared at Varya and Sagun in disbelief. No thing could have confused or hurt him more than these words. After all, it was Varya's voice and only hers that called him from the man's camp. From the first night he heard her music, he was certain that she sang only for him. She wanted them to live together in the wild. And not once was Sagun's name mentioned.

The black dog smiled at him and said, "You're not strong enough to run with Varya, pup. Why, after a lifetime of man-food, you will be lucky to keep up with the weakest member of my pack!"

And Kam-Yuk looked at the wild dogs around him and saw that all were young and lean and strong. Sagun barked, "Follow me, pup! It's time you tasted a dog's true meat—the food of the wild."

The black dog led him across the meadow and into the woods. The pack followed them with Varya at their head. Sagun took him to a place where the snow was colored red with blood. There lay the remains of a bull elk. The pack had killed it in the night.

This was Kam-Yuk's first taste of wild meat, and it was good. In fact, he had never tasted anything so good in his entire life. He only wished there had been more of it. But the pack had already stripped most of the meat from the bones. While he ate, Sagun watched, nodding his huge head now and then in approval. The rest of the pack found places in the snow to curl up and sleep. They paid no more attention to Kam-Yuk, which was a great relief to him.

When the young husky tore the last scrap of flesh from the elk bones, Sagun raised his head and gave a frightening howl. The wild dogs jumped to their feet and formed a long line behind him. Kam-Yuk saw the pack was ready to move, so he decided to follow his beloved Varya. He trotted right up behind her, but to his surprise she spun around suddenly and bit him hard on the cheek.

"You stink of the man's camp!" Varya snarled. "Go to the rear of the pack where you belong. Only the strongest dogs can run at the head."

A tiny trickle of blood ran down the side of the young husky's face. But the pain of the wound was not half so great as the pain he felt in his heart from being driven away by the creature he loved so much.

Kam-Yuk slunk to the rear of the pack with his tail between his legs. As the line of dogs loped into the forest he fell in beside a big husky who had one blue eye and

23

one brown eye. They trotted up a narrow trail to the crest of the mountain, then down the other side toward a distant valley. The farther they went the better Kam-Yuk felt.

"I am new to the wild," he said to himself. "Perhaps if I eat more wild meat I'll grow larger and stronger and won't smell so much like the man's camp. Then Varya will want me!"

The pack traveled through the mountain forest for many hours. All around were towering pine trees. The sky was clear and blue. Streams of melted snow sparkled in the sunlight. Kam-Yuk breathed the clean, cold air and listened to the voices of the birds as they called to one another in the treetops. He had never felt so free, and that made running with the wild pack seem worthwhile, even though he wished that he could be alone with Varya. But as they ran, Kam-Yuk began to notice something strange about One-Blue-Eye, his companion. Every few steps, the dog would wince as though he was in pain. Once he stumbled over a big rock in their path as though he had not seen it. Obviously, something was wrong with him.

Several hours later when the pack stopped to rest, One-Blue-Eye rolled onto his side and began to shiver all over and whine softly. Kam-Yuk sat by him and asked, "What is the matter? Are you hurt?" One-Blue-Eye raised his head and said hoarsely, "I was the first to corner the bull elk last night during the hunt. It gored me with its antlers. Something is injured deep inside my chest."

Kam-Yuk came to his feet instantly and said, "I'll run and tell Sagun! Perhaps he can help you."

"No! No!" the big husky whispered desperately. "You aren't in the man's camp anymore, pup. The rules of the wilderness are different. Say nothing!"

They did not rest for long. Thirty dogs followed Sagun's voice, and with so many stomachs to fill, the pack had to stay on the move in search of game. Mile after mile they loped down the mountainside, alert for the scent of deer, elk, or moose. And One-Blue-Eye grew sicker with each step. Tiny drops of blood began to gather around his mouth and nose. Now and then he would yelp softly with pain. Kam-Yuk felt terribly sorry for him. But he did not know how to help him.

Finally, when the pack reached the deep valley at the foot of the mountain, One-Blue-Eye fell into the snow and did not get up. This was too much for Kam-Yuk. He dashed through the pack causing great alarm and confusion among the other dogs. When he reached the front, Sagun turned on him angrily and snarled, "What are you doing? Go back where you belong!"

"But someone is hurt!" cried Kam-Yuk. And he told the leader how One-Blue-Eye had been injured and that he could no longer keep up with the pack. Sagun looked up the trail behind them and saw the wounded dog. One Blue-Eye struggled to his feet for a moment. But as soon as he took a step, he fell again into the snow.

Sagun only watched for a few seconds. Then he said, "Too bad. When he cornered that elk last night, he served the pack well. But we must leave him here."

"You can't!" cried Kam-Yuk. "He is hurt. He needs help!"

The hair on Sagun's back bristled. His eyes glowed savagely at Kam-Yuk. "What I do is for the good of the pack. We need food, and there is no time to wait for one sick dog."

Kam-Yuk looked at the other faces around him and

pleaded, "Won't anyone help him?"

Sagun roared, "Are you challenging me for leadership of the pack?"

Kam-Yuk ran from him in terror.

"Then take your place in line and let's get going!" the black leader snorted after him.

Off the pack ran, even faster than before. It was as though Sagun wanted to quickly lead the other dogs out of sight of One-Blue-Eye.

Kam-Yuk let the others troop by until he spotted a familiar face. It was the dog who once had appeared in the man's camp and told him stories of the wilderness. The young husky joined the line and drew alongside him. "What do you think will become of One-Blue-Eye?" Kam-Yuk asked.

"I don't know," said the other. "A bear or a wolverine will probably get him."

"That is terrible!"

The wild dog only grunted as though the matter was of no concern to him. "We all have to go sometime."

"Can't anything be done?"

"I remember you from the man's camp, pup," the animal said with a sly smile. "I'll tell you a secret about the wilderness. Here, your life is important only to you. So watch out for yourself, and don't worry about any other dog. Because if anything happens to you and you can't serve the pack, you'll end up like him!"

Kam-Yuk dropped to the end of the line and looked over his shoulder at One-Blue-Eye. The animal was no more than a dark spot on the snow far behind them. Kam-Yuk remembered the day his father had died and trembled. The young husky was glad Roc had not come to such an end, cold and alone in the middle of an endless

wilderness.

At that instant, a new feeling was born in Kam-Yuk's heart—the fear of death.

Another snowstorm swept across the Yukon that night. In front of it came a terrible Arctic wind. The dogs buried themselves in snowbanks to escape the bitter gale. But even that did not help. All of the pack suffered badly from the cold. But Kam-Yuk suffered worse than the others. He was used to warm blankets and a cozy wooden hutch. He shivered so hard that he could not sleep.

Things were even worse when the pack took to the trail the next morning. Snow was so deep that the lead dogs had to take turns breaking a path for the others to follow. The bitter wind whipped first one way, then another, and kept them from finding food . For no sooner did they smell game than the wind shifted and made them lose the scent.

Kam-Yuk was not only tired from constant running and little sleep, he was also hungry. The few scraps of meat he had been able to tear from the elk did very little to quiet his growling stomach. So when the pack discovered a small deer which had fallen into a deep snowdrift, he felt relieved.

Quickly Sagun and Varya killed the animal and dragged it from the snowdrift. Kam-Yuk leaped in to grab a piece of meat. Instantly, the black leader and his mate turned on him. They bit his nose and neck and threw him onto his back. When Kam-Yuk scrambled to his feet, Sagun snapped savagely, "Wait your turn! It is for the good of the pack that the strong eat first. We must break trail and hunt game"

But by the time it was Kam-Yuk's turn to eat, there was nothing left of the small deer but a few bare bones.

He chewed one desperately. He knew that he must eat soon or he would not have strength to keep up with the pack.

Sagun did not let them rest for long. The deer was so small that no wild dog ate much. The pack began the hunt once more. They moved as fast as they could through the heavy snow. Always their noses were alert for the scent of game. But there was nothing to be found. Another day passed. Then another and another. Kam-Yuk felt a growing weakness in his legs. But he remembered One Blue Eye lying alone in the snow, and the fear of death drove him on.

Still, if the pack had not found the man's hut, Kam-Yuk might have starved. It was just a tiny wooden shed on the side of a mountain. But inside, there was food. Kam-Yuk knew the strange smell of the hut from the man's camp. It was a place where supplies were stored. He reasoned that the man must have built this hut for his long hunting trips in the mountains.

The door was chained and locked. But Sagun and some of the stronger dogs went to the back of the shed and tore at a plank with their teeth until it broke. Then they squeezed inside and dragged out pieces of smoked deer meat wrapped in cloth.

Kam-Yuk counted the pieces. There was not enough for everyone, which meant he would be left out again. Suddenly an idea came to the young husky. He noticed the pack ate only those things that still smelled of the wild. So, when Sagun and the others were not looking, he crept around to the hole in the back of the hut, slipped in side, and searched for the dry meal which the man fed his dogs. There was only a little scattered across the frozen floor. He snuffled the pieces up, found two small wooden boxes and gnawed them until they broke open. Inside were hard biscuits. He quickly gobbled these down. He wanted more, but the storehouse was empty.

For some reason, Kam-Yuk felt safe inside the old shack. But he knew Sagun must not catch him there. He crept outside, making sure that no one spotted him. Once he reached the safety of a small fir tree he looked around and saw the strangest thing happening. Sagun and Varya were going from dog to dog ordering each to drop his food and sing about the terrible cruelty of the man. Kam-Yuk slipped over to the wild dog he knew and asked, "If the pack hates the man so much, why do they eat his food?"

"If we didn't, sooner or later, hunger would make us turn on one another," the dog answered in a whisper. "The pack would destroy itself."

The pack slept that night around the man's storehouse and moved at daybreak. As usual, Kam-Yuk was in the rear. But today, he did not run alone. A dog slipped from his normal place near the middle of the pack and fell back beside him. Kam-Yuk saw immediately that the animal was weak from starvation. Like him, this dog had got no more than a bone from the deer, and he had had none of the man's meat. Watching him stagger on the wilderness path made Kam-Yuk thankful for the handful of meal and hard biscuits.

The pack stopped again at midday to rest. Kam-Yuk saw the starving dog disappear under the snow-covered branches of a spruce tree. He hoped the poor animal would not be left behind like One-Blue-Eye.

Suddenly there was a loud snap! As one, the pack sprang to its feet and ran to the spruce tree, howling furiously. Kam-Yuk followed. He had no idea what had

30

happened, but the closer he came to the spruce tree, the stronger became the scent of man.

The starving dog was alive and unhurt. He was inside an iron cage. There was a dish of dried fish and meal beside him.

Sagun broke through the crowd of dogs and shouted, "You fool! You have let yourself be trapped by the taste of man's food. You have betrayed us!" And his entire body trembled with rage.

"You should have starved to death like a true wild dog," howled Sagun. The pack members tore at the cage with their fangs while the hungry dog cowered inside. Kam-Yuk, knew the pack would have ripped him in pieces if it could have reached him. But the cage was too strong.

The young husky remembered Half-Wolf and wondered if this was how he had been taken from the wild. Perhaps he had also grown tired of hunger and cold and let himself be caught in a trap baited with man's food. Kam-Yuk almost wished that he could find another cage with a dish of dried fish and meal for himself. But there was no chance to search for one. Sagun screamed, "To the man's camp!" and the pack was off.

Kam-Yuk waited long enough to whisper to the caged dog, "Don't worry. You'll be all right. The Brothers of the Sled will find you." And the frightened, starved animal smiled at him weakly.

The young husky thought they were close to the man's camp, and he was right. By nightfall the pack stood on a high bluff overlooking it. Kam-Yuk could see sled dogs moving around the man's cabin. Suddenly he longed to play with old friends and spend a night curled up in a warm blanket. But how could he? He saw what

31

had happened at the cage. The pack would never let him leave. And even if they did, he knew the man would never for give him for running away.

Sagun growled angrily, "We lost a traitor. But another will soon take his place. Varya will teach those mongrels in the man's camp a lesson!" And he ordered the pack to be quiet while his mate raised her voice in song.

It was the same song Kam-Yuk had heard when he lived in the man's camp. But for some reason, it no longer sounded so wonderful. In fact, the longer Varya sang, the more her voice bothered his ears. He began to wish that he was strong enough to make her shut up.

Then, suddenly, Kam-Yuk heard another song on the night wind. It came from the man's camp. The notes could barely be heard over Varya's voice. It was terribly sad. It sprang from the throat of a dog in great pain. When he realized who it was, Kam-Yuk's blood ran cold, and he began to tremble. His mother! She was crying for her child lost in the wilderness.

What happened next could not have been helped. All of the fear, the cold, the hunger, and the loneliness of the last few days poured out of Kam-Yuk. He raised his nose toward the starlit sky and let out a mournful howl. Instantly, Varya rushed at him. She sank her fangs into the loose skin on the side of his neck and shook him until he screamed for mercy. Her white face was filled with hate. "You ruined my song!" she snarled. "If you ever do that again, I'll rip out your throat!"

From the man's camp, there came the noise of a great commotion of some kind. Sled dogs were barking. There were war cries in the air. As Kam-Yuk cowered in the snow under Varya's feet, he could not help but wonder if the teams of Uther and Half-Wolf were again fighting.

"Let's go!" cried Sagun angrily, and instantly the wild dogs were on their feet and running. But this time it was Varya who led the pack. Sagun ran at the rear, right behind Kam-Yuk. Now and then, the young husky felt his hot breath and heard an awful rattle in his throat. The pack ran faster and longer that night than ever before. The muscles in Kam-Yuk's legs ached. But he knew that he must keep up with them, and he must not stumble. For if he did, Sagun would certainly kill him. It was during this terrible flight from the man's camp that Kam-Yuk reached a decision. He simply decided that he hated Sagun and Varya more than he did the man.

"If I am going to die anyway," he said to himself, "it is better to die under the whip and club of the man. At least he has some mercy. He might give me a bowl of food before he kills me."

By dawn, every dog in the pack was ready to drop from exhaustion. They had to stop. The wild dogs fell into the snow and slept for an hour. Then Sagun left Kam-Yuk alone and took his place at the head of the pack. The endless hunt for food began once more.

Kam-Yuk had an idea. The other dogs did not know of the biscuits and meal he had eaten in the storehouse. So he pretended to be much weaker with hunger than he really was and started lagging farther and farther behind the others. Now and then, he even stumbled over a limb or a stone the way One-Blue-Eye had. Finally, the last member of the pack disappeared over a low hill. It was his chance for escape! The young husky turned and ran as fast as he could in the opposite direction.

For a time he followed the winding tracks of the

pack, but he thought the man's camp was somewhere to the east. So he left the trail, even though he knew the fresh snow would slow him down. He was already tired from the long night's run, and his lungs ached with each breath he took. He wanted to lie down and sleep. But whenever the young husky felt that he could not take another step, he closed his eyes and remembered how it felt to have Sagun running at his heels. Fear gave him strength.

Deep snowbanks and dangerous cliffs often forced Kam-Yuk to change directions. And, since he had not lived for very long in the wilderness, he soon lost his sense of direction. More than once his heart sank when he crossed his own trail and discovered that he had traveled in a wide circle. By afternoon the young husky began to wonder if he would ever find a sign of the man's camp. Then he bolted from the dense forest into a broad moun tain meadow and saw, far to the east, a thin ribbon of smoke rising from the chimney of the man's cabin. Instantly he knew that this was the place where he first joined the wilderness pack.

Kam-Yuk raced toward the man's camp. But no sooner did he reach the center of the mountain meadow than a savage howl stopped him in his tracks. Suddenly, from behind a large boulder, Sagun leaped into his path, and the wild pack burst from the forest on all sides. The young husky had stepped into a trap.

Sagun walked up to him and asked with a smile, "Where do you think you are going? A young pup shouldn't wander alone in the wilderness."

"I don't want to belong to your pack anymore," cried Kam-Yuk.

"It's not as easy as that," replied the black dog.

34

Kam-Yuk now knew that all hope was lost. He would never reach the man's camp. But he decided not to die quietly like One-Blue-Eye. He gathered all the courage left inside him and snarled loud enough for the other dogs to hear him, "Sagun, you are a liar!" Sagun's mane bristled. "You say the man is cruel. But who is worse, you or him? At least in the man's camp the weak, the old, and the sick are cared for. But there is no room for those in your pack. That is why all these dogs are so young. Only the young or strong can live for very long in the wilderness! And you are a cheat! You let Varya sing for you because you know a dog would never come to the sound of your awful voice. And you are a fraud! You say wild dogs are true brothers, but you know they would kill and eat each other if you didn't let them steal man food!"

The entire pack held its breath and waited to see what Sagun would do. No one had ever before stood up to him.

It was Varya who spoke first. "Didn't I tell you we should have killed this pup in the beginning?"

Sagun nodded his black head calmly, "And I should have listened to you," he said. "No matter. He will be food for the pack today." And the black dog shouted, "Kill him!"

The pack swarmed over Kam-Yuk, howling and biting. He tried to fight, but there were too many. He was driven into the snow under their weight. Long fangs cut his face and back and sides. Cruel jaws sank into his hindquarters, tearing muscle and bone. Then Sagun leaped in and caught him by the throat. Kam-Yuk could not breathe. He began to slip into a deep darkness, where there was no more pain or noise or slashing teeth.

Then Sagun let him go, and all around there were cries of fear and hate. Feet trampled him. There was much savage snapping of jaws. Kam-Yuk thought that he must be dreaming, because a name was suddenly called that he felt he had not heard in ages—Uther!

Slowly, the light returned to Kam-Yuk's eyes. With that light came terrible pain, and the young husky knew it was no dream. Above him stood the great black and gray leader of the sled dogs. And beside Uther was Kam-Yuk's mother and the seven other huskies of Uther's team. These nine dogs had formed a tight ring around the wounded pup. Circled about this ring was a much larger one formed by Sagun and his thirty.

The black dog stood a few feet from Uther, trembling with rage. Part of his left ear was missing.

Uther took a step toward Sagun and said, "We have come for Kam-Yuk."

The leader of the wild pack was in such a rage that foam dripped from his mouth. He roared, "Never! He is ours!"

"Not anymore, Sagun. We heard his voice last night. He called for us. He called for the man. And we are here to take him home!"

"You are here to die!" snarled Sagun.

Uther's mane bristled and he answered, "The man is with us. Go back into the wilderness, Sagun. If you fight us now, he will take your life!"

"I'm not afraid of the man. What can he do but build dog pens and cabins and chain dogs to sleds? You are his strength. Without you, he is nothing!"

Uther replied, "You've lived in the wilderness too long, Sagun. You don't know the power of the man's fire and musket. He leaves you in peace because he hopes to bring some of your pack to the camp and teach them to be sled dogs. But if you fight, he will be forced to kill you to protect us."

"Don't listen to him," howled Varya to the pack. "What are they to us?" Kam-Yuk's mother answered her coldly, "If you touch my son, I am your death!"

Varya cursed her with every foul name she knew. Then she said, "There are three of us for each of them."

But no sooner did those words leave Varya's throat than from the rear of the wilderness pack came the sound of fighting. The ring of wild dogs split. Through the gap came Half-Wolf with his belly close to the snow, his jaws snapping first to one side and then to the other. And at his heels were the eight huskies of his team. The inner circle of sled dogs grew twice as large.

Half-Wolf took a place at Uther's shoulder and growled, "Count again, Varya. The Brothers of the Sled have gathered!"

Sagun screamed at him in hate. "Half-Wolf! You traitor! You left us for the man's camp. You are a coward and a weakling!"

"Am I a weakling too, Sagun?" asked Uther. Or have you forgotten that when you were just a puppy, I was leader of the pack?"

Nothing Kam-Yuk had ever heard startled him more than those words. In his head, he could see Half-Wolf running with the pack, but not Uther. And he certainly could not imagine Uther as a beast like Sagun.

The moment Uther said this, something seemed to snap inside the black dog's head. Sagun raised himself on his hind legs and screamed, "Kill them! Kill them! Kill them all!"

Then, he lunged straight for Uther's throat. But before he could reach the leader of the Brotherhood, something stopped him in midair. He looked like a dog who had run full tilt to the end of a rope and been jerked short. The mountain trembled with a thunderous noise. Sagun fell backward into the snow and lay on his side— dead!

The wild dogs fell into confusion. They had no idea what had happened to their leader. Some thought lightning might have struck him, yet there was not a cloud in the afternoon sky. But the sled dogs knew the sound. It was the roar of the man's rifle. He was standing in the trees with his musket. And when he saw Uther in danger, he shot Sagun.

Uther bellowed the war cry. "The man is with us!"

And Half-Wolf howled, "Fight, Brothers! FIGHT!!!" And the inner circle of sled dogs broke out in all directions.

The sled dogs were still badly outnumbered, but two things stood in their favor. First, Sagun was dead, and the wild dogs took their orders from him during a fight. Second, whereas the pack was weak from hunger, the sled dogs were well fed. It was true enough that the man's food had little taste, but it was good for them, and pulling the sleds had made them strong.

On all sides of Kam-Yuk, the battle raged. Uther's fury was a terrible thing to see. No dog who challenged him stood for long. Most ran away in fear when they saw the flame in his eyes. Half-Wolf fought with the cunning of his wild cousins. Every time a wild dog lunged at him, he quickly stepped to one side, and the animal's jaws snapped shut in the air. Then Half Wolf would leap in and slash a face or shoulder to the bone. But the fiercest fighter of all was Kam-Yuk's mother. She had found Varya in the confusion of the battle, and the two clashed so savagely that no other dog dared to come near them.

Kam-Yuk wanted to help. But he was too badly crippled to move. Then a wild dog suddenly leaped over him and landed squarely on Uther's broad back. The leader of the Brotherhood was knocked off his feet. He fell into the snow under his enemy's paws. Things might have gone badly for Uther if the wild dog's tail had not dangled above Kam-Yuk's head. The young husky grabbed it between his teeth and locked his jaws. The wild dog yelped with surprise. He twisted around and bit Kam-Yuk's side. But the young husky would not let him go—not until Uther was up. Then Uther grabbed the wild dog by the back of the neck, lifted him into the air, and shook him from side to side like a puppy would shake a rag. When he let him go, the wild dog ran away screaming in terror and pain.

Suddenly, a member of the wild pack cried, "Away! Away! Run for your lives!" And the wild dogs ran for the safety of the forest with the man's huskies at their heels. Kam-Yuk was left alone.

The pain in his body grew so great that he closed his eyes and whined softly. Then something stirred nearby. He looked and his heart sank. There stood Varya. Her white fur was soaked with blood. She limped toward him, dragging her right foreleg.

"They left me for dead," she growled in a voice that sounded as though it belonged to a snake and not a dog. "But as you can see, I am not dead." She tottered for an instant as though she would fall. "You're the cause of this, pup. You are the reason my mate is gone. And for that you will pay with your life."

Varya hobbled toward him. Kam-Yuk knew that he could not defend himself. All he could do was lie in the snow and watch Varya come for him and wonder how he ever could have loved such a wicked, ugly beast.

But Varya did not reach him. Her body was suddenly lifted into the air as though by a great gust of wind. She grunted loudly and was thrown back into the snow. Again the mountainside shook with the thunder of the man's rifle. Varya lay very still, her head resting upon the neck of her mate, Sagun. A bullet had pierced her evil heart.

Kam-Yuk twisted this way and that searching for the man. He appeared at the edge of a pine forest to the east. The man raised a hand to his mouth and whistled softly. Kam-Yuk heard his name called. In that instant, all of the hatred he once held for the man seemed to vanish. The young husky felt a great need to run to the man and leap into his arms. But his legs were crippled and his body torn. He could do no more than kick and roll about in the snow. The pain became too great for Kam-Yuk. He closed his eyes and howled weakly. Then darkness swept over him once more.

In that darkness, he dreamed that the man's arms were lifting him into the air. He heard the man's voice, and though he did not understand the words, he knew they were neither cruel nor angry. They spoke of warm beds and food and healing. Then a deeper darkness took him.

It was the trail song of the Brotherhood that woke him again. The sled dogs were singing a new verse.

"Sagun, poor Sagun, you lost your way.
And with your poor Varya, your beautiful mate.
Musket and fire you did not understand:

40

Those things are part of the power of man.
You forced him to send you to early graves,
    When the lives of his dogs he had to save.
But two from the wild have this day been led,
    And they will be Brothers, brave Brothers,
Strong Brothers, oh, they will be Brothers of the Sled."

Kam-Yuk opened his eyes and found that he was riding on Uther's sled. He was wrapped in warm blankets as white as the Yukon snow. The man had cleaned his wounds and set his injured legs in splints and tied him to the sled with leather straps.

In front of Uther was Half-Wolf's sled. The man stood on its runners. In its bed was the iron cage with the starving wild dog inside. He had also been saved from the wilderness.

The Brothers were happy and sang at the top of their lungs. Not one of their number was lost in the fight on the mountain. And Kam-Yuk had returned to them.

It was strange, but the more the young husky listened to the trail song of the Brotherhood, the less he could remember of Varya's music. What little he could recall seemed very ugly and stupid. That night the two sleds reached the camp, and Kam Yuk was taken to the man's cabin where he was fed and given a bed near the fire. Months passed before his wounds healed and he could again walk about the camp. But by spring, he was strong enough to be given a place in Uther's team.

As the years passed, Kam-Yuk grew to become a mighty sled dog. It was said of him that no creature ever lived who had a greater heart. He could pull a sled harder, carry his load longer, and defend the man more fiercely than any husky in the Yukon Territory. If all the stories

41

of his adventures and daring deeds were written down, they would fill a book much larger than this one.

The day came when Uther left the team for a quiet pen beside the man's cabin. Kam-Yuk was made the leader of his sled. And all of the puppies born in the man's camp saw him as a great hero and wondered at the deep scars he bore on his neck and legs. But mostly they wondered why he would leave the camp one night each winter and go to the bluff high above it to sing. Sometimes his voice was sad. Often it was very fierce. But always it was clear and loud.

"We are the Brothers of the Sled;
By the powerful hand of the man we are led.
No snow too deep, no path too long,
No weight too heavy to silence our song.
Shoulder to shoulder and heel to toe,
Hunger and fear we never shall know.
Dogs of one heart may it always be said;
For we are the Brothers, the Brothers, the Brothers . . . Oh, we are the Brothers of the Sled!"

"The Brothers of the Sled" and Real Life:

Many of you who read this tale were raised in the church the same way Kam-Yuk was raised in the man's camp. Like Kam-Yuk, you may find there are some things about God's camp you do not like. And sooner or later, a beautiful voice will call you. Varya can take many different shapes and colors. But her music is the same. She will tell you God is cruel. She will say Christianity puts chains on you and you should leave God's camp behind.

I know that I heard her voice. And just like Kam-

43

Yuk, one day I followed it. But when I joined those who did not believe in God or Christianity, I quickly learned the same lessons Kam-Yuk did about the wild pack. Only God sees every person as important. In the world you are only important to yourself. If you cannot serve the world, the world will leave you behind the way the pack left One Blue Eye.

Beautiful words and great ideas may lead you away from God. But the world is cruel. There is no place for weakness There is little room given for disagreement. And there is certainly no comfort to be found for trouble or sickness or death. In fact, if people in the world did not steal virtues like kindness, mercy, goodness, and peace from God's camp, they would tear each other to pieces.

Well, one lonely night, I called for help just like Kam-Yuk; and God sent Christians to help me. I learned two things about them. First, their food was the Bible and it made their hearts strong. And second, God protected them.

Don't be fooled by Varya the way Kam-Yuk and I were. In the world, you will find only fear and a terrible hunger of the heart. In God, there is comfort and strength.

Matthew 11:29-30—"Take my yoke upon you, and learn of me; for I am meek and lowly in heart: and ye shall find rest unto your souls. For my yoke is easy, and my burden is light."

How the Raccoon Saved His Life

Deep in the Ozark Mountains of Missouri, there once stood an ancient oak tree. This was no ordinary oak tree, the kind you and I find when we hike through the woods. The animals say this was the oldest and largest oak that ever grew in the Ozarks—or in any other mountains, for that matter. It was two hundred fifty flaps of a mockingbird's wings from bottom to top; and a squirrel would hop thirty times to get around its thick trunk at the bottom.

Of course, that is the way animals measure distance in the Ozark Mountains. But in case some of you are not very good at animal arithmetic, the oak was about one hundred sixty feet high and eighteen feet around by man's scale. This giant stood like a king in the middle of a mountain valley. No other trees grew near it.

The animals in that part of the Ozarks tell many stories about about that tree. But the most famous of all is the tale of a young raccoon who once lived among its branches.

On the day this adventure happened, only two animals had homes in the oak—the raccoon and an old, fat opossum. Usually, many creatures lived there, but it was late summer. By this time of year the birds had left their nests, and very seldom did squirrels bother to visit because, in spite of its great size, the old tree produced few acorns and those were eaten quickly. Now and then a woodpecker stopped to hunt for bugs under the bark of the oak. But that was all.

The raccoon and the opossum thought this tree made a fine summer home, however. These two animals hunted for food at night. During the day they wanted to sleep in a cool, safe place. Well, the old oak tree had plenty of leaves for shade. It was so tall and had so many branches that their enemies, like the bobcat, had a hard time climbing it, much less finding their dens. So both of them set up housekeeping in hollow places toward the top of the tree.

The raccoon and the opossum lived very peaceful lives until one afternoon when the young raccoon awoke suddenly from a deep sleep. He felt terribly afraid. But of what he was afraid he had no idea. He poked his head outside the doorway to his den and looked all around. Nothing. He hopped onto a nearby limb and scampered up and down its length, searching the ground below the tree and the sky above it. But if he had heard or smelled an enemy in his sleep, he certainly did not see one now. The longer the young raccoon remained outside, the deeper his fear became. Finally he crawled to the highest limb of the tree. From that spot he could see above the tops of all the other trees in the valley. The forest was strangely still. Not a bird or an insect was chirping in the brush. On the horizon he saw a mass of black clouds. Forks of lightning flashed beneath it. A summer storm was coming.

"I have been through many storms before," the young raccoon said to himself. "I wonder why I feel so afraid now?"

Just then, he remembered the opossum. "Perhaps the opossum will know what the trouble is."

Down the oak tree the young raccoon scampered. He found the hole that led into the opossum's den, stuck his head inside, and chirred loudly. He almost got his nose bitten off. Animals hate to be startled, and opossums can be especially nasty when they are surprised and sleepy. But the young raccoon was very quick. He jerked his head away an instant before the opossum's jaws snapped shut.

"Wait!" he cried. "It's me, the raccoon." When the opossum's eyes finally got used to the bright light pouring through the doorway to his den, he recognized the young raccoon's black and gray face. He hissed, "What's the matter with you? Can't you see it's daylight outside? Leave me alone. I am trying to sleep!"

The opossum rolled onto his back, scratched his big belly, and closed his eyes again.

"Don't go back to sleep!" cried the young raccoon.

"Why not?" grumbled the opossum.

"We are in danger!"

The opossum's eyes popped open. He stirred and sat up slowly, propping his back against one wall of his den. "What do you mean?" he asked.

"Is there a bobcat about?"

"I don't think so."

"A mountain lion?"

The young raccoon shook his head. "No. I'm sure I would have seen an animal that big."

"What then?" growled the opossum.

The raccoon hopped onto a nearby limb and again searched the ground under the tree. Then he turned to the opossum and chirred nervously, "I don't know. I woke up a few moments ago with the feeling that I was in terrible danger. I ran all around the top of the tree looking for enemies. But the only thing I saw was a thunderstorm in the distance."

The opossum grunted loudly and stuck his head out the doorway of his home. "You woke me up just to tell me that?"

The raccoon nodded at him.

"That is the silliest thing I've ever heard," the opossum snorted. "Go away and leave me alone."

"No, please," the raccoon begged. "You must help me. I have never felt like this before, and I don't know why. Can you tell me what the trouble is?"

The old, fat opossum sighed deeply and once again rolled onto his back. Lying like that, he made a loud wheezing sound every time he breathed. "My guess is that you won't leave me alone until I answer you," he said with a great yawn. "All right, I'll tell you what the problem is—you don't know how to use your head!"

The young raccoon scampered to the doorway of the opossum's den and looked inside curiously. "I don't understand."

"I am sure you don't," the opossum answered. "All of you raccoons are the same. You try to think with your feelings instead of your heads."

The opossum closed his eyes and a wide grin spread across his face. "But not me. I trust my nose and eyes and paws and ears—and especially my head. If I can't figure something out in my head, then I know it isn't worth worrying about!"

"But something frightened me," cried the young raccoon. "What was it?"

"A bad dream," grumbled the opossum in reply. "Yes. I am sure that is the answer. You had a bad dream, woke up, and thought you were in danger."

"But I don't remember dreaming about anything. Besides, I have been wide awake for a long time, and I am still frightened."

The opossum grunted in disgust. "Hmph! Well, it looks like the only way I am ever going to get any sleep is teach you how to use your head. Answer this. Since the moment you awoke, have you heard or seen or smelled an enemy?"

"No," said the young raccoon honestly.

"And tell me, when raccoons are frightened, where do they run for safety?"

"To a tree."

"And isn't this old oak the biggest and strongest tree in the mountains?"

The young raccoon nodded. "Then you are safer here than any place in this valley. Now, go back to sleep and leave me alone!"

"But a storm is coming!" the raccoon cried. "What if we are in danger from the storm?" The opossum grinned again. It made him look very sly. "You still aren't using your head, raccoon. Tell me, how old do you think this tree is?"

The young raccoon answered, "I don't know. It has stood in this valley for so long that no animal can remember when it wasn't a full grown tree."

"Exactly!" snapped the opossum. "So, it has been through thousands of summer storms, yet it still stands." The opossum reached out and patted the wall of his den. "Yes. Lightning may scorch this old tree. The wind may break a few of its branches off, but it will be here for our grandchildren to live in."

The young raccoon looked around nervously and said, "I guess you are right."

"Of course I am," the opossum replied. "Now, go back to your den and sleep. It was all a bad dream. Nothing more." The young raccoon slowly climbed the trunk of the oak to his home. He crawled inside the hollow and onto his bed of dry leaves and twigs. He shut his eyes and tried very hard to go to sleep again. But the longer he lay there, the more terrified he became.

He tossed and turned. He listened to the rumble of the thunder. The storm was nearly to the valley now. The wind was blowing hard, and the old oak tree began to sway and creak. Finally, he could not stand it any longer. He left his den and climbed down to the ground.

The storm clouds overhead were blacker than any he could ever remember seeing. He scampered into the surrounding woods. For some reason, the farther he ran from the old oak tree, the better he felt. In a few moments, he reached a small creek where he often hunted for food. He hopped onto a fallen log that stretched over the stream and started to cross. Just then he heard the sound of digging. Dirt flew into the air from a hole in the bank of the stream. Now, if raccoons are anything at all, they are curious. So he ran over to the hole to investigate.

He peeked inside and a pawful of dirt hit him right in the face. "Hey!" he sputtered. "Be careful."

Out of the hole popped the striped head of a large badger. The badger looked the young raccoon up and down. Then, without so much a "Hello," he scooped up the loose dirt he had just tossed out of his den and patted it around the mouth of the hole. Then, he popped back inside.

More dirt flew from the little cave. When the badger came back outside, he was pushing a large rock with his nose. He put it right in the opening to his den and packed more dirt around it.

"If you aren't careful, you are going to close the door to your den," the young raccoon warned.

The badger disappeared for an instant When his head popped up again, he said, "That is just what I intend to do. Now, go away!" And down he went.

The young raccoon became very curious when he heard that. He crawled up to the hole and again stuck his head inside. But the badger growled at him and tried to chase him away.

"Leave me alone!" snapped the badger. "Can't you see I'm busy?"

"But why are you trying to shut yourself inside your little cave?"

"Because I have a feeling that I'd better do it! That's why!" the badger grumbled and, instantly, he was gone. More dirt flew from the hole.

"But what could make you want to do such a strange thing?" cried the raccoon, who stood on his hind legs a few feet from the hole.

Pop! The badger's head appeared once more. "I don't know," he said. Pop! He was gone. The young raccoon kept a safe distance. He knew badgers could be fierce fighters if they were teased or bothered too much.

"But that is silly," he chirred loudly.

"Why?" asked the badger from deep inside his hole.

"Because the opossum told me feelings aren't important! All you can trust are your eyes, nose, paws, ears, and head. But mostly your head. You should never bother yourself with things you can't figure out in your head."

"Hm!" The badger grunted when he came back up to pack more dirt around the doorway of his home. "Is that what the opossum really said?"

The raccoon nodded.

"I'm surprised he has lived to be as old as he is," said the badger, and he vanished again.

The raccoon heard the badger digging very hard. He shouted above the noise, "Why do you say that?"

The badger shoved another stone, twice as big as the first, into the opening and stopped to catch his breath. He put one paw on the stone and said, "Listen and tell me what you hear, raccoon!"

The young raccoon turned his head from side to side. The only sounds echoing though the valley were peals of thunder and the rush of wind through the treetops.

"Just the storm. That is all I can hear," he replied with a trembling voice, because a deep fear suddenly caught hold of him again.

"Where are the rest of the animals who live in this valley?" asked the badger.

And suddenly the young raccoon remembered that he had neither seen or heard another creature except the opossum since he first woke up that afternoon. "I— I don't know," he answered.

The badger snorted, "I'll tell you where they are.

54

They are hiding in burrows and ditches and caves for the same reason I am sealing myself inside my den! They are afraid!" And again the badger dived into his home and began throwing dirt into its entrance. The opening was growing much smaller now. When the badger came up for the last time, he could just squeeze his head through the hole.

The young raccoon cried to the badger in despair. "But why? Why should you be afraid of something you cannot see or touch or smell or even work out inside your head?" The badger hissed urgently, "Listen to me quickly, young raccoon—that is if you want to grow up to be an old raccoon. Do you believe the opossum is the only animal in the whole valley who can think? Don't be silly! But most of the animals in this valley know there is something they can see and hear with besides their eyes and ears. We have a word for it, raccoon. Instinct. It makes our feelings strong and warns us of danger. And my instinct tells me something terrible is about to happen in this valley."

Just then, lightning struck nearby and there was a loud crack of thunder. Rain began to fall. The young raccoon knew he must find a safe shelter. At first, he started to run back to his home in the oak. But the awful fear rose inside him and he stopped.

Suddenly, he remembered an old, fallen tree. He had discovered it one night while hunting for food. The thick trunk was hollow, and it was not very far away. The raccoon dashed across the stream and up the steep hill on the other side. At the top, he found the log. The hole in its center was just big enough for him to squeeze inside.

No sooner did he back into the hollow log than the

storm hit the mountain valley with all of its terrible fury. Rain poured from the sky. Lightning flashed everywhere, and the thunder was so loud that the earth trembled. Now and then, hail rattled against the outside of the log. Then the young raccoon heard a noise from the sky that was completely strange to him. It was a roar, a whistle, and a howl all rolled into one awful scream. He stuck his head outside and looked up through the rain. The black clouds overhead had taken an odd shape. They looked just like a monstrous, twisting snake. The cloud snake reached down toward the mountain valley and passed right above his hiding place.

The young raccoon backed into the hollow log as far as he could. Never in his life had he seen a tornado. It was more frightening to him than any bobcat or mountain lion could ever have been. Then came a loud *crack!* Wood was being ripped apart by the power of the whirlwind. The raccoon covered his ears with his paws and shut his eyes. He trembled in fear.

The cry of the tornado quickly faded into the distance. But the rain swept the mountain valley for an hour. The poor little raccoon was so scared he did not move again until nightfall. When he heard the frogs and crickets singing in the woods, he nervously crept from the log. He trotted down the hill and back toward his den in the oak tree.

But as soon as he reached the clearing at the middle of the mountain valley, the young raccoon stopped in surprise. The giant oak was no longer standing where it should have been. Its limbs and thick trunk were twisted and broken into thousands of pieces. The whirlwind had torn it apart. Strangely, the powerful tornado touched nothing else in the valley, as if the storm had come for that one tree. The raccoon searched the wreckage of the oak tree for the opossum. But he had vanished without a trace. The animals of the Ozark Mountains say that the tornado snatched the opossum from his den and carried him away into the sky.

"How the Raccoon Saved His Life" and Real Life:
One day, you are certain to run into somebody like the old, fat opossum. He trusted the old oak tree. His head told him the tree was much too strong to be broken by a summer storm. But his "good sense" did not save him. Men who are like the opossum want to believe this world will go on forever and ever. They do not want to hear what the Bible says about a terrible storm that will one day sweep man's world away.

2 Peter 3:10—"But the day of the Lord will come as a thief in the night; in the which the heavens shall pass away with a great noise, and the elements shall melt with fervent heat, the earth also and the works that are therein shall be burned up."

The young raccoon saved his life because he followed his instincts. He left the oak before that tornado destroyed it. People also have instincts planted deep inside them. God put them there to draw men and women to Himself and safety. Our instincts tell us there is far too much on this earth that cannot be explained outside of God. They let us know that something very important is missing in our lives when God is not there. And they warn us that the world we live in is not what it ought to be and one day God is going to make it right. Those instincts are the reason so many millions of people seek God.

Lemmings

There is a vast country that lies between the Arctic Circle and the North Pole. Early explorers named it the tundra, a word that means "barren land." Seldom is the tundra very warm. Strong winds sweep its grassy hills and plains all year long. There are terrible blizzards during the winter. Frost can cover the earth in any season. And even though the sun never dips under the horizon during the two short months of summer, it seldom gets warmer than fifty degrees.

If you could fly from your bedroom and soar across the Arctic tundra on the warmest day of the year, you would probably look around and wonder, How on earth could any animals live here to tell stories about? You would not see a single tree, just grasses and moss and tiny Arctic flowers and small shrubs hardly three feet tall.

The low plains would be dotted with shallow bogs, streams, and lakes, for the melted snow cannot sink very far into the ground. The earth just a few inches beneath the top of the tundra is frozen solid, even on the warmest summer day.

But the look of the tundra can fool you. In reality, many animals live there. Flocks of birds build nests on the tundra. Herds of reindeer and caribou cross its wetlands, and they are followed by packs of wolves. Near the coastline of the Arctic Ocean you might find polar bears, seals, and walruses. Many of these animals range far south when the cold winter comes, but the creatures of this story live in the tundra the year around—musk oxen and lemmings. And if you searched high and low in this great wilderness, you could not find two animals who are stranger or more wonderful or more different from one another.

Musk-oxen may stand as tall as six feet from the bottom of their hooves to the top of their humped shoulders, and they can weigh nine hundred pounds. They have long, dark hair that almost drags on the ground, and they travel together in herds, grazing upon the grass and moss of the tundra.

Musk-oxen have a strange habit. Whenever they become frightened, they form a tight circle around their young. Then they lower their heads and the points of their big, curved horns bristle in all directions like spears. No wolf or bear is foolish enough to attack such a dangerous fort as this. Lemmings, however, are so small that you could hold one in your hand. They have very short tails and look a little like a hamster you might buy in a pet shop. Most are gray or brown. But some turn snow white in winter. They tunnel through the shallow soil and build homes in the cracks between rocks.

It so happens that lemmings have a very strange habit too. Every now and then they gather in great numbers and travel across the tundra. It is said that a need for food starts their long journeys. But once the migration begins, lemmings may pass through fields where there is much to eat, yet they touch little. In spite of their small size, they can travel several miles in a day. And they allow nothing to stop them. It was this last fact that a young musk-ox had to learn one autumn day.

This musk-ox belonged to a great herd of nearly a hundred animals. All summer long, he and his friends and family had wandered across the tundra eating as much of the coarse grass as they could find. They were storing fat for the long Arctic winter, which was almost upon them. Because there were so many musk-oxen in this herd, they had to travel great distances in order to find enough food for everyone. So it happened that one day the herd reached the edge of a steep cliff that overlooked the sea.

Now the young musk-ox had never seen the ocean in his life. It struck him with wonder. He stood near the edge of the rocky cliff and smelled the salt air. He listened to the sound of the waves and to the calls of the sea birds as they flew this way and that over the churning water and broken flows of ice.

Suddenly he heard a soft rustle in the grass beside his hooves. He looked down, and a brown lemming darted to the edge of the steep cliff. Of course, the young musk-ox had seen lemmings before but seldom scampering around in the open during the middle of the day. They usually searched for their meals when it was darkest on the tundra. He wondered what the little animal could be doing. But before he had a chance to open his mouth and ask, the brown lemming leaped over the edge of the cliff and fell from sight!

The musk-ox snorted in surprise. Carefully he crept forward and peered over the edge of the rocky cliff. Its terrible height made him dizzy. Far down below, foamy waves crashed against the rocks. The tiny lemming was nowhere to be seen.

Even while he stared down at the ocean in confusion, three more lemmings darted from the grass beside him. Then, one after the other, without so much as a whistle or a bark, each of them hopped over the edge and fell down the steep face of the cliff. They vanished into the swirling water and never appeared again.

The young musk-ox backed away from the cliff in horror. He shook his hairy head from side to side and pawed the earth. He could not understand why the lemmings would have done such a thing. He thought they had all gone mad.

Just then a *fifth* lemming bounded into the open along the same trail taken by the others. But before he could leap over the cliff to his doom, the musk-ox bellowed, "Wait! Wait! What are you doing?"

The lemming turned his head slowly and studied the musk-ox for a moment. Then he whistled. "I am following the trail of those who went before me, of course."

"But if you jump from the top of this cliff you will surely die!"

The lemming's tiny face grew angry. He barked, "You only say that because you are a musk-ox!" Then, without another word, he also leaped over the edge of the cliff.

The young musk-ox could not believe his eyes Surely any creature in its right mind could see that a fall from such an awful height into deep, icy waters meant death. The musk-ox was determined to learn the answer to this mystery. He sniffed out the track that the five lemmings had taken to the cliff and stood over it. A few moments

61

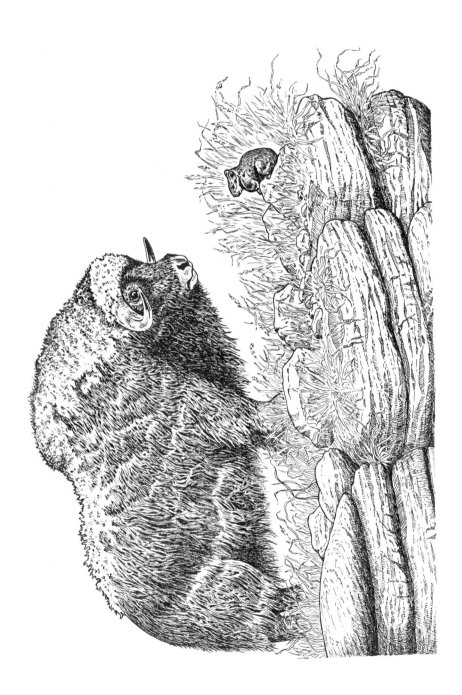

later, another lemming appeared right in front of him. The little animal was nearly exhausted from his long journey across the tundra. His gray fur was matted and ragged.

The musk-ox barred the lemming's path. Whenever the lemming tried to run around him, he would lower his huge head and stomp the earth with his hooves to frighten the animal back.

Finally the lemming hopped onto the top of a small rock. He cried angrily, "What do you think you are doing? Get out of my way! I must follow the trail of those who went before me!"

"No, I won't," grunted the musk-ox. "If you follow their trail, you will fall into the water and drown!"

The tiny lemming gave a shrill whistle, which is the way he had of laughing at someone. Then he barked, "You only say that because you are a musk-ox!"

"What do you mean?"

"Are musk-oxen good swimmers like we lemmings are?"

"Of course not," the musk-ox replied. "But no matter how good a swimmer you are, you could never cross such a great distance as this. And besides, there is a high cliff just a few feet in front of you. If you were to fall from it, I don't think you would ever have a chance to do any swimming."

Again the little lemming whistled loudly. "Nonsense," he said. "You only say that because you are a musk-ox! Answer this. Are musk oxen afraid of heights?"

"Yes."

"Do musk-oxen have very good eyesight?"

"Well, no, but I can see well enough to know that what is in front of you is no stream or lake. It is much too wide and rough for a creature as small as yourself to cross."

The lemming piped, "Why should I believe you? After all, you admit that you have poor eyesight and you are not a good swimmer and you fear high places. Fear makes all things look different from the way they really are. So I don't believe this cliff you saw is really very high, nor is the water any deeper or wider than some streams and rivers I have already crossed. Now, get out of my way!"

The young musk-ox became terribly upset. He bellowed, "Can't you see that I am only trying to save your life? Why must you follow the path of the others?"

"They were the first to set out for the new land," replied the lemming. "I must follow their tracks if I am to reach it."

"What new land? What on earth are you talking about?" asked the musk-ox.

"At the end of my journey lies a wonderful country where there is plenty of food, lots of room for a lemming to burrow in the ground, and no enemies to hunt us. I don't know exactly where it is. But it is not very far from here. I am sure of that!"

"The end of your journey is only a few feet in front of you," snorted the musk-ox. "If you leap over the edge of that cliff, you will die like all the others. Listen to me, lemming. There is enough food around these cliffs for many of your kind. You needn't go any farther.

Live here!" When the little lemming heard this, he became so angry that he hopped up and down on the rock. "You only say that because you are a musk-ox!" he cried. "Your kind are always wandering around this cold tundra trying to make everyone believe they should

be happy here. Instead, you should be like us and seek a better land. If you just traveled far enough, you would find it."

"Listen to me," the musk-ox pleaded. "My herd has wandered far and wide. Never have we seen such a place as you describe. And besides, a creature as small as yourself couldn't travel far enough in a lifetime to leave the tundra. It is much too big!"

The lemming shut his eyes and squealed furiously, "You only say that because you are a musk-ox!" Then he darted between the young musk-ox's legs. This caught the big animal by surprise. While the musk-ox stumbled around in confusion, the little gray creature raced to the brink of the cliff. He stopped and shouted in triumph, "If you had any brains inside that thick head of yours, you would follow me!" Then the lemming leaped into the air and fell toward the raging waves that broke against the rocks below.

The young musk-ox stepped slowly to the cliff and looked down its steep face. He bowed his head, sighed deeply, and replied, "You only say that because you are a lemming."

"Lemmings" and Real Life:

Some people refuse to believe in God. They say, "We know why people believe in God. Life is often full of sorrow and pain. People are afraid of the troubles they may have to face and need something to make them feel safe. When they were children, they had parents to protect them. So, they dream up a 'Heavenly Father' who will watch over them and love them and care for them throughout their lives. Inside their heads, people lean on God the way a man with a hurt leg leans on a crutch. But God doesn't really exist. He is only a dream." That is what some people say.

If ever you hear something so foolish, remember the story of the musk-ox and the lemming. After all, the lemming thought he knew why the musk-ox said he was in danger. But that did not prove a thing. He really was in danger! You see, just because somebody thinks he knows why someone else believes something, does not necessarily mean that what that person believes is not true.

What the musk-ox said was true. It was the lemmings who were wrong. In their minds they had a good reason for wanting to leap into the sea. But they were wrong.

"You only say that because you are a musk-ox!" the lemming cried.

The young musk-ox replied correctly. "You only say that because you are a lemming."

Proverbs 26:5—"Answer a fool according to his folly, lest he be wise in his own conceit."

When Chipmunks Fly

Chipmunks are happy animals for the most part. They enjoy playing all kinds of games like tag or hide-and-seek or king-of-the-log almost as much as they like to eat. And chipmunks love to eat. But once there was a young chipmunk who never played any games. His name was Bubo. And for the longest time, he was the saddest little chipmunk who ever lived in the mountains of eastern Tennessee.

Now Bubo was not unhappy because he was sick or hungry or lonely. In fact, just the opposite was true! He was just about as healthy as a chipmunk could be. He lived a very safe life in a part of the mountains where there were dozens of oak trees just loaded with tasty acorns and few foxes to chase him. And there were lots of other chipmunks living in the woods around his home. They would have played with Bubo any time he wanted. But he never felt like playing games.

The problem was that Bubo did not want to be a chipmunk. He did not like scampering across the dark, damp forest floor or digging his burrow underneath a fallen log. Bubo wanted to have bright, beautiful wings and soar high above the mountains in the clear blue skies. Bubo wished with all of his might that he could become a bird!

Sometimes Bubo would sit for hours under the branches of a small cedar tree near the edge of a high cliff. He watched the birds floating high above the treetops. He daydreamed about changing into one and being carried above the mountain peaks by the gentle winds. And whenever Bubo dreamed like this, he always crawled back into his home beneath the fallen log even more unhappy than he had been when he awoke that morning. He would curl up sadly in his bed of grass and whisper to himself, "If only I knew a secret that would change me into a bird. I would do anything to learn how to fly. Anything! I don't care how hard it might be."

Then one morning, while Bubo was searching for acorns under a big oak tree, he heard a loud snap high above him. He looked up. At the very top of the tree, he spotted a tiny squirrel dangling from the end of a broken branch. Suddenly, to Bubo's great surprise, the squirrel let go of the branch. Down he fell! Faster and faster he dropped. Then suddenly the squirrel spread his paws wide apart. His body became a small furry square with a round head on one end and a thick tail on the other. The wind lifted him up again and he floated safely to the next tree.

Never in his life had Bubo seen a flying squirrel. He had no idea that these little animals were born with soft flaps of skin along their sides that caught the wind like a sail and helped them glide through the air. Bubo thought that a squirrel had actually learned to fly. And that made him squeal with joy! After all, squirrels were a lot like chipmunks. So if a squirrel could learn how to be like the birds, then he could too.

Bubo ran to the next tree and shouted excitedly,

69

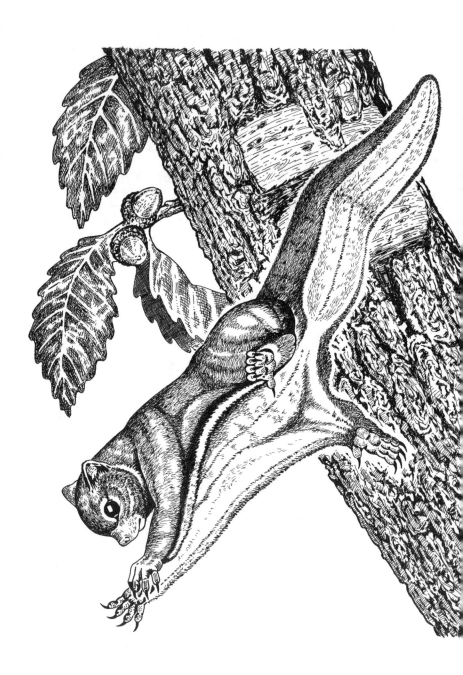

"That was wonderful, just wonderful!"

Taken by surprise, the flying squirrel looked down at Bubo and barked, "What are you chattering about, chipmunk?"

"You flew!" cried Bubo. "You flew just like a bird! You have learned their secret. Please tell me what it is. I want to be like a bird too. I hate living down here."

Now, any other animal in the woods might have laughed out loud to hear a chipmunk say something so silly. But not this flying squirrel— at least not on this particular day. Just hearing the word *bird* made him angry. Earlier that morning the little flying squirrel had crawled too close to a bluejay's nest. The mother jay thought he was trying to steal her eggs. She rapped him between the ears with her sharp beak and chased him from the tree. Just thinking about it made the squirrel's whiskers twitch with rage.

As soon as the flying squirrel heard Bubo cry "bird," his fur stood on end. He squealed loudly, "Learn to be like a bird? Why a bird is just a dirty little animal with feathers that builds nests and eats worms. That is all a bird is!" And the squirrel plucked a small acorn from a nearby twig and tossed it at Bubo. He was trying to hit the chipmunk but the acorn missed and fell into the grass at the foot of the tree.

The flying squirrel leaped into the air once more and glided toward another tree. As he floated away, he chattered angrily, That's all they are! Just dirty little animals with feathers that build nests and eat worms!" He did not even hear Bubo crying after him. "Oh, thank you! Thank you for the fine acorn. And thank you for telling me the secret of how to be a bird. It was so simple after all! Why didn't I see it before?"

Bubo had no idea that the flying squirrel was angry at him.

Bubo ate the acorn, and when he saw three other chipmunks playing nearby he ran to join them. For the longest time, they chased each other around and around the trunks of trees in a game of tag. The other chipmunks wondered about the change in Bubo. Usually he was so very sad. Now he seemed to be the happiest creature in the forest. And they really became confused when Bubo suddenly stopped and whispered to them, "Do you want to hear a secret? Birds are just dirty little animals with feathers that build nests and eat worms," and then scampered away into the woods.

But Bubo could have cared less at that moment what any other animals thought of him. There was just too much work to be done.

Off he ran. He knew just where a family of bobwhites took an afternoon nap under a blackberry bush. He hopped right into the middle of the sleeping birds and shouted, "Can I have some of your feathers?"

Well, it is not hard to imagine what happened next. The startled bobwhites flew away from the blackberry bush in all directions. Poor Bubo. He was nearly beaten silly by the wild flapping of their wings. But when the dust settled and the birds were gone, Bubo opened his eyes, and there at his feet were six of the finest feathers he ever saw. He gathered them carefully in his mouth and carried them to his hiding place under the cedar tree.

Next, Bubo ran through the woods collecting sticks and grass and thin pieces of tree bark. He brought these back to the cedar tree and began weaving them into a nest.

You might think that a chipmunk would find building a nest a difficult chore. But not Bubo. He had spent so much time watching birds do it that in a couple of hours he had knitted the finest little nest under that cedar tree you could imagine.

Next came the hardest thing Bubo ever did in his life. He found a pile of damp leaves on the forest floor. He scratched and scratched until he uncovered a long, fat, red worm. The red worm wiggled this way and that under his paws. Bubo curled up his nose in disgust. He stood there watching it for the longest time. Then, quicker than a chipmunk can say,

"I am on a tree stump,
    To me an acorn bring;
And if you cannot chase me down,
    I'll always be your king!"

(and little chipmunks can say that pretty fast when they play king-of-the-log), Bubo ate the fat, red worm. He gobbled it up from head to tail—or tail to head, he could not tell the difference. One thing is for certain. Birds may love the taste of a fat, juicy worm, but not chipmunks. Chipmunks eat nuts and seeds and berries. To Bubo the red worm tasted awful. He felt sick. He crawled slowly back to the nest he had built under the cedar tree and lay on his back for the longest time groaning and moaning.

It took several hours before he felt well enough to stand up again. In fact, the sun was just about to dip below the western rim of the mountains when Bubo crawled out of his nest and scampered to the edge of the high cliff in front of his cedar tree. The sheer wall fell

73

straight down two or three hundred feet Another chipmunk might have run away in fear. But not Bubo. He just looked over the edge and grinned happily.

"I am almost done," he said to himself proudly. "Now, what was it the squirrel told me? Oh yes, birds are just dirty little animals with feathers that build nests and eat worms. Of course that is the truth. How silly of me not to see something so simple. And now that I have some feathers and I've built a nest and—ugh—eaten a worm, all I have to do is get real dirty, and I'll be just as good a bird as any sparrow that ever flew in these mountains." Bubo rolled over and over in the dirt. When he was about as filthy as a chipmunk can possibly get, he scampered back to the cedar tree and carefully collected his bobwhite feathers. With one in each of his four paws and two in his mouth, he hopped to the edge of the cliff once more. He could not remember ever being so happy. He was sure that he was soon to become the world's first flying chipmunk.

With one great leap, Bubo was over the edge of the cliff. He spread his little legs wide apart just like the flying squirrel had done. And then he flapped the feathers in his paws as hard as he could. But to Bubo's great surprise, he was not carried away upon the wings of the mountain wind. He did not fly or soar or dip or glide. In fact, what he did could not even be described as a very good dive. Bubo just fell! He fell like a rock torn from the edge of the towering cliff. He fell end over end. He fell faster and faster. Down, down, down. Bubo lost two of his precious bobwhite feathers when he opened his mouth to scream in terror.

There was no doubt about it. If Bubo had kept on falling as fast as he was falling and then hit the valley

floor below, there would have been one less chipmunk in the Tennessee mountains. But at the very last second, his life was saved by a pair of mockingbirds. Well, maybe it was not so much the mockingbirds as it was their nest.

A father and mother mockingbird had discovered a fine young birch tree growing from the face of the sheer cliff. They decided it was a perfect place to build a home. It was far enough from the ground that snakes or weasels could not climb up to it and steal their eggs. A curve of the cliff face protected it from strong winds. And the thick mass of leaves would keep the rain or hot sun from bothering their children. So the mother and father mockingbird found the strongest limb of the tree and built their nest in one of its forks. And to tell you the truth, it was the finest nest they had built in their entire lives. Just about the time Bubo leaped from the top of the cliff, the father mockingbird placed the last stick on the nest and he and his wife stepped back to admire their work. "Perfect!" the father mockingbird cried with great pride. "There is no better nest in the mountains."

"Yes," his wife sang cheerfully. "It will stand up to any thunderstorm."

"And it is safe from all of our enemies," the father bird replied.

The two mockingbirds tried and tried, but they could not think of a single thing that could threaten their new home. Not once did the thought pop into their heads that their nest might be in danger from a flying chipmunk.

While the birds stood there admiring the fruit of their long hours of work, Bubo suddenly streaked down from the sky like a great hailstone. Through the leaves of the birch tree he fell and *plop!* he landed squarely in the center of their magnificent nest. Twigs, grass, feathers, and leaves flew into the air—and so did the startled mockingbirds. The birch tree shuddered from top to bottom, and the limb that held the nest sagged down and down until it seemed certain that it would break in half. But instead, the bottom of the nest gave way, and Bubo tumbled into the top of a small pine tree just a few feet below. Down through the limbs of the young pine the little chipmunk bounced. Finally he landed on the ground with a thump. Poor Bubo just lay there very, very still for the longest time. The fall had knocked the wind out of him. His little body was battered and bruised from head to tail. It hurt him just to wiggle his nose! He kept his eyes shut tight. He did not know if he was alive or dead and was afraid to look and see.

But he was very much alive. The mockingbirds' soft nest and the springy limb of the birch tree had saved his life. They had acted like a safety net, slowing his terrible fall.

Suddenly Bubo heard loud chirping. He gathered his courage and opened one eye. There stood the two mockingbirds on the ground beside him. They were scolding him with all their might and ruffling their feathers furiously.

"You ruined our home!" cried the mother mockingbird.

"It took us days to build it," squawked her mate. Now we are going to have to start all over again!"

"Where on earth did you come from anyway?" asked the other.

Bubo carefully felt himself all over. He was greatly relieved to discover nothing was broken. Slowly, he stood up. His little legs quivered from fright.

"I—I'm terribly sorry," he said with a trembling voice.

"I didn't mean to ruin your nest. It was an accident. I was trying to fly. But when I jumped off the cliff, for some reason I couldn't do it."

The pair of mockingbirds stared at him in disbelief. "You tried to fly?" asked one in surprise.

"Why on earth did you do that?" piped the other. "You are a chipmunk, not a bird. Chipmunks can't fly."

"But the squirrel I met this morning said I could!" Bubo replied. "He told me that birds are just dirty little animals with feathers that build nests and eat worms. So I gathered some feathers, built a nest of my very own, ate a worm, and rolled in the dirt until I was very dirty. But when I tried to fly like a bird, I fell from the top of the cliff."

The mockingbirds started to laugh. They laughed so loud and so hard that a dozen other birds came to see what was the matter. And when the mockingbirds told them what Bubo had done, they began to laugh as well.

Finally Bubo got angry. "You are mean!" He pouted. "That fall might have killed me, and all you can do is laugh."

The father mockingbird cried, "But thanks to our nest, you weren't killed! And how can we help but laugh? We can't imagine anyone being silly enough to believe that chipmunks can fly."

A tiny bluebird began to feel sorry for Bubo. He flew to a nearby branch and chirped, "Listen, chipmunk, I could tell you ten thousand different things we birds do, and if you were able to copy them all, you would still not be one of us. You can never have the heart of a bird. That is a much greater thing than the nests we build or the food we eat or the feathers we grow!"

The pair of mockingbirds flew to the top of the pine

tree and one of them turned to say, "We have a lot of work to do, rebuilding our nest. But before we go, we'll leave you a proverb that might keep you alive a while longer, chipmunk. 'There is nothing in the world so simple, as a creature who thinks everything is simple.'" And the mockingbirds flew back to the birch tree on the side of the cliff and once again began to build a nest in its branches. One after the other, the rest of the birds flew away as well. Soon just Bubo and the tiny bluebird remained. The bluebird said to the little chipmunk, "If ever you decide to fly again, please come tell me first. Then I can warn my friends to build their nests on another mountain!"

But Bubo never again tried to fly. In fact, from that time on, he even stopped daydreaming under the cedar tree. And very soon, he was happy and playing games like all of the other chipmunks in the forest. His friends wondered what had happened to him. But they were polite and never asked. And Bubo never told them.

"When Chipmunks Fly" and Real Life:

Sooner or later, you are going to hear people say some pretty silly things. One of them may come up to you and say something like, "Man is just a few ounces of chemicals and a lot of water! That's all a man is!" Or another will try and tell you, "Man is nothing more than a very intelligent animal!" Well, if you believe them, then you are just as foolish as Bubo when he believed what the flying squirrel told him about birds.

Oh, it is true enough that a man's body is made up of a small amount of chemicals and several gallons of water. But if you took those same chemicals, placed them on a tabletop and poured an ocean of water over them, you could not make a man. And man is intelligent, all right. But that does not explain how man happens to have a conscience, believing some things are good and others are evil. No other creature on the face of the earth has that. Nor does it explain why man creates beautiful art, music, and stories. Remember, the flying squirrel did not actually lie to Bubo. Birds do have feathers; birds can be quite dirty; birds build nests; and birds eat worms. But Bubo discovered the hard way that birds were much greater than those few things. Likewise, man is also much greater than chemicals or water or intelligence.

The Bible tells us man is a very special creation of God. In Psalm 8:4 and 5 we read, "What is man, that thou art mindful of him? and the son of man, that thou visitest him? For thou hast made him a little lower than the angels, and hast crowned him with glory and honour."

As you get older and read more about the history of men on this earth, you will quickly discover that evil people always believe man is less wonderful than the Bible says he is. Then they do not have to feel bad for committing terrible crimes against others. "After all," they say, "if a man is just a very smart animal, why should I be bothered about what I do to him? Whales are smart too, and we hunt them!"

But the truth is that man is greater than all the physical things that we put together and call a human being. God gave man an eternal soul. That is why man is so valuable in God's eyes. That is why God sent His only son, Jesus Christ, into the world so man's soul could live forever in His loving presence.

John 3:16—"For God so loved the world, that He gave His only begotten Son, that whosoever believeth in Him should not perish, but have everlasting life."

The Heart of the Mongoose

Once, when there were no engines to power boats, only the wind and canvas sails, men from Europe crossed the ocean in wooden ships and discovered the islands of the Caribbean between North and South America. They found that the soil on these islands was wonderful for growing sugar cane. Very soon, great sugar plantations were carved from the tropical jungles. But these jungles were filled with poisonous snakes. So men went to India, caught mongooses, and brought them to the Caribbean islands.

Now a mongoose is a little creature that looks something like a cat and very much like a weasel. It is the natural enemy of a snake. Whenever a snake and a mongoose meet, a terrible fight is almost certain to occur.

In the Caribbean, the mongooses were raised as pets. They lived outdoors, roaming around the plantation grounds, battling any snake they found.

But because the mongooses were born in a distant land, they were very different from the creatures native to the islands. And it did not take the birds of the Caribbean very long to learn how different they could be.

It seems that several families of little yellow sugarbirds once lived in a tangle of sea grapes and mangrove bushes that grew near a great house built by the owner of a sugar plantation. Every spring the birds would build their domed nests among the vines and branches and lay their eggs. These bushes had been their home for many generations.

One day, while most of the sugarbirds were away from their nests searching for food, they heard a shrill cry for help from one of the flock who remained behind to watch the nests. Quickly they flew back to their homes. There, coiled around the branches of one of the shrubs, was a deadly pit viper. It had inched its way from the ground to one of the lower nests and eaten all three of the speckled eggs inside it.

The sugarbirds were furious. They darted this way and that, screaming at the snake, trying to chase it away. But the pit viper was not concerned. His cold eyes could freeze a bird with fright if it came too close, and he knew there was nothing they could do to hurt him. Even if they pecked with all their might, they could not injure his heavy scales.

Slowly the snake made his way down the trunk of a sea grape bush to the ground. As he slithered into a small hole he had discovered among its tangled roots, the sugarbirds heard his terrible voice. "Tas-s-sty eggs-s-s-s. Nic-s-s-s-e little tas-s-sty egg-s-s. I am going to like it here. Yes-s-s-s."

The birds were terrified. What were they to do? Their nests were not safe with the viper living under the bushes. One and all they flew to the highest branches and held a council. It was noisy and full of fear and doubt.

"What are we to do?" wailed the little yellow faced bird who had just lost her nest to the pit viper.

"Yes," said another. "If this snake keeps eating our eggs, there will be no children to sing with us next year."

"We must do something to make him leave!" cried a third. "But what?" asked another. Suddenly the leader of their flock cried for silence. When the frenzy of bird voices finally grew quiet, he chirped. "I think I have the answer! All of you agree we aren't strong enough to fight the pit viper by ourselves." The other birds chirped in assent. Then we must find someone else to fight him for us. And I think I know who!"

"Who is it? Who?" asked the other birds excitedly.

"The mongoose!"

That threw all of the others into confusion. They knew very little about the mongoose. After all, the man who lived in the great house had only recently brought the animal to his plantation.

"What do you mean?" asked the others.

"I was flying near the man's house yesterday and saw the strangest sight that any of you could imagine. I saw the mongoose fight and kill a small green tree snake on the wide, grassy clearing near the banyan grove."

"A green tree snake is not a deadly pit viper!" cried one bird.

"But if he can kill one snake, perhaps he can kill another! What have we to lose by trying?" asked their leader. "If he is strong enough to kill the viper, we could build a bed for him right under our bush to keep him here. He could protect us from all other snakes!"

There was a general chirping of assent from all of the other birds except one, a tiny hummingbird who had only recently begun to build her nest in the branches of the sea grapes and mangroves. But since she was not a sugarbird, she lived apart from them and seldom got involved in their affairs.

But now the tiny hummingbird suddenly darted into

the air above the low bushes and piped, "No!"

"Why not?" asked the bright yellow leader of the sugar birds angrily.

"Because I have seen the mongoose too," replied the tiny hummingbird as she hovered above him. "Each time I have flown to the man's house to drink from his flowers, I have stopped to watch that strange little animal. I don't believe he has a heart! And I don't intend to place the future of my children in the paws of a beast with no heart."

"Nonsense!" cried the leader of the sugarbirds. "Certainly the mongoose has a heart. After all, he killed a snake didn't he?"

"Yes! Yes! He must have a heart, a very good heart!" replied the others.

The hummingbird chirred loudly. "All that proves is that the mongoose may hate snakes. But if he does not have a good heart, if he cannot tell the difference between right and wrong, or if he doesn't care, then he will bring as many problems with him as he takes away."

"Well, what do you think we should do about the viper, then?" asked the sugarbirds. "After all, some of us have already laid our eggs, and the viper is eating them!"

The hummingbird cried, "Wasn't it the man who brought the mongoose to these islands? Let us see if we can lead the man here. He might still use the mongoose to kill the viper, but I am certain the man has a good heart. He could protect us if the mongoose does not have one."

Now, those words caused a great stir among the other birds. They feared the man. He was huge. He was unlike any other creature they had ever seen. He had the power to clear broad stretches of jungle and turn it into sugar cane fields. They could not understand his strange language.

"No! No!" all of the other birds cried noisily. "Only a fool would trust the man. He is far too different from other creatures. We must see if the mongoose can save us!"

"There," said the leader of the sugarbirds in triumph. "Everyone agrees with me. We shall trust the mongoose.

"You can trust him if you like. But not me!" the hummingbird answered. "If you intend to bring the mongoose here, then I shall leave and find a safe place to build my nest—a place free of pit vipers and mongooses!" Then the hummingbird flew from the tangle of sea grapes and man grove limbs into the surrounding jungle.

The sugarbirds gathered closely together and worked out a plan. They decided to send their leader to find the mongoose and tell him of the hole where the viper lived. If the mongoose agreed to come and if he killed the snake, then they would make for him a bed of soft grass and sticks right under their nests.

The yellow sugarbird flew as fast as he could to the man's house. He darted from tree to tree and rooftop to windowsill searching for the little animal. Finally he spied the mongoose sleeping in the shade of the banyan trees near the long porch of the great house. Down he flew to a branch just above the mongoose's head.

The small bird studied the furry little creature carefully. The mongoose was lying on his back with all four paws dangling limply in the air. The tips of his white fangs gleamed from beneath his upper lip. The yellow bird noticed with a shiver that if it were not for the mongoose's short legs and narrow face, he might have easily mistaken him for a cat. And the sugarbird was terribly afraid of cats.

Perhaps the hummingbird is right, he said to himself nervously. *Maybe the mongoose does not have a good heart.* Then and there, the bird decided that before he led the mongoose to his home in the bushes he would try to find out for certain.

The sugarbird chirred loudly and awakened the sleeping mongoose. The animal opened its eyes and stared curiously at the bird above him.

The bird said, "Excuse me, friend mongoose, but there is something I want to ask you." The mongoose just lay very still but did not answer.

"I don't want to make you angry," said the bird. "But I've heard it said that a mongoose has no heart. Is that true?"

The mongoose seemed to come to life suddenly. He rolled this way and that in the dust beneath the banyan tree "That is silly," said the mongoose. "Of course I have a heart!"

The yellow bird became very excited and flitted a little closer to the mongoose. "Would you say that you have a good heart?" he asked.

"A good heart? I should say not," replied the mongoose. "I have a wonderful heart—the best of any creature on this island!'

The sugarbird was overjoyed. "I thought so!" he cried happily. "Since you have such a good heart, perhaps you would be willing to help me and my friends. There is a pit viper living under the bush where our nests are built. If we cannot find some way to kill him or drive him away, he will eat our eggs."

No sooner did the sugarbird say the word *snake* than

86

the little mongoose's ears pricked up and he rolled onto his small feet.

"I saw you kill a snake yesterday," the yellow bird said hopefully. "I know that this viper is very dangerous, but if you are not afraid of him, would you come with me and fight him for us?"

The mongoose shook the dust from his fur. Then he looked up at the sugarbird and said, "Let me have a look at this snake of yours."

Off the bird flew with the tiny mongoose scampering as quickly as he could across the ground below in pursuit. In a little while, they reached the place where the dense sea grapes and mangroves grew. The yellow bird perched upon a branch above the viper's hole. All of the other sugarbirds flocked around him and watched the mongoose carefully.

The little animal stretched his long body over the carpet of fallen leaves and sniffed deeply. No sooner did he smell the oily scent of the pit viper than his eyes seemed to flash a deep red for an instant. The fur along his back bristled. Suddenly he began to bounce all around the tangled roots of the bushes on stiff legs, stamping his feet in a strange dance. A chirring noise rolled from his throat. It was the war chant of a mongoose.

"Hi, snake! Ho, snake!
　　Come up, come up and fight me, snake!
I am the mongoose fast and strong,
　　You are the viper deadly and long.
Hi, snake! Ho, snake!
　　Come up, come up and fight me, snake!"

Something in that odd sound made the viper furious, for he instantly raced out of the hole, raised his ugly head high into the air, and began to rock from side to side. His tongue flicked in and out as he studied the little mongoose carefully.

"What is-s-s this-s-s little beas-s-st?l' the snake hissed loudly, but he was only talking to himself. "I have never s-s-seen anything like him before. I hate the nas-s-sty s-s-sound he makes-s-s. But when I bite him, he will not make that s-s-sound anymore!"

When the sugarbirds heard the voice of the pit viper, it chilled them with terror. They were so afraid they could not even move. They sat upon the branches above the snake like little painted statues.

Suddenly the viper coiled and struck at the mongoose. But the little animal quickly leaped to one side and hid behind the thick vine of a sea grape. The pit viper drew back hissing to himself with astonishment. "I mis-s-s-sed him! I have never mis-s-s-sed before!"

The mongoose began to back slowly away from the big snake. Angrily, the viper slithered after him. Now he was more determined than ever to kill the mongoose. Three times the deadly pit viper coiled and lunged at him, and three times the mongoose jumped beyond the reach of the snake's deadly fangs.

In dismay, the sugarbirds watched as the mongoose retreated from the snake. They thought he was afraid and was running away. But this was untrue. The mongoose was a very cunning fighter. He did not want to battle the dangerous viper among the tangled vines and branches of the sea grapes and mangroves, where he had little room to move.

The mongoose drew the viper outside of the bush to a flat, bare place in the sun. No sooner did the viper slither into the open than the little animal began chanting his war cry again.

"Hi, snake! Ho, snake!
    Now, the game is over, snake.
Coil and strike with all your might,
    For here the mongoose plans to fight!
Hi, snake! Ho, snake!
    Now, the game is over, snake!"

The pit viper hissed at him in hatred and struck as hard and as fast as he had ever struck at another creature in his life. But the mongoose was faster. Straight up into the air the little animal leaped. The snake's poisonous fangs touched nothing but the emptiness beneath him. And when the mongoose came down, his tiny paws landed squarely on the snake's neck, pinning him to the ground. Instantly, the mongoose reached for the viper's V-shaped head. He sank his teeth into the tough scales just behind the snake's skull. He locked his jaws and held on with all his might.

The snake twisted this way and that trying to wrench himself free. And when that did not work, he coiled around the mongoose's long body and tried to squeeze the air from his lungs.

But the mongoose would not let him go. Tighter and tighter he closed his jaws. The warring pair rolled over and over in the clearing and thrashed about so wildly that soon the air was full of dust and the birds could no longer see what was happening. But then everything grew still once more. The dust began to settle, and the sugarbirds saw the mongoose dragging the long pit viper toward the man's house. He had won the battle. The snake was dead. The sugarbirds cheered and cheered.

That very afternoon they began flying into the nearby jungles gathering twigs and grass, which were placed on the ground underneath the bush. In no time at all they had woven a huge nest for the mongoose. They sent their leader out the very next day to find him. When the two of them returned to the bushes, the mongoose curled right up in the nest and went to sleep. The sugarbirds were overjoyed. Finally, they had a champion to defend them from snakes.

The mongoose seemed content with his new home. The grassy bed was very soft, and the shade of the sea grape and mangrove leaves kept him cool during the heat of the day. He stayed there for many days.

The little sugarbirds laid more eggs that year than in any other season they could remember. Their nests were filled with speckled eggs. And they were so confident in the power of the mongoose to protect their eggs that they no longer bothered to keep a watcher in the bushes when they flew around the island searching for food.

One day, the leader of the sugarbirds was flying over the cane fields and spied another viper sunning itself on a flat rock. Immediately, he turned and flew to fetch the mongoose. He darted into the dense branches of the sea grapes and mangroves. The bushes were quiet, for all of the other sugarbirds had gone into the jungles. He landed upon a thin vine and looked around curiously. Something did not seem right to him. Then, to his great horror, he saw that every nest in the bushes was broken and thrown to the ground. And there was the mongoose sleeping on his soft bed of grass surrounded by the broken shells of all the sugarbird eggs.

The little yellow bird wailed loudly, "What have you done?"

The mongoose slowly opened one eye and looked at him. What do you mean?' he asked sleepily.

"You have eaten all of our eggs!" cried the sugarbird. "Yes, and they were very good, too," the mongoose said with a yawn.

"How could you have done such a thing?"

"Oh, it was easy really," the mongoose said, stretching himself all over and rolling out of the bed and onto his feet. "I just crawled through the branches very carefully. Then, I knocked the nests to the ground and rolled the eggs over to my bed."

The sugarbird screeched, "What kind of a beast are you? Don't you have a heart?"

The mongoose stood on his hind legs and looked curiously at the little yellow bird. "I answered that question the day I fought the viper, didn't I? Of course I have a heart—a very, very good heart. It pumps blood through my whole body. In fact, I never knew a mongoose with a bad heart. Why, if our hearts didn't work so wonderfully, we could never kill vipers. Our small bodies would not be strong enough or fast enough."

Hearing the loud cries of their leader the rest of the sugarbirds returned to their home in the bushes only to find their nests and eggs gone. They too began to chirp and wail in sorrow. Soon, the noise became so loud that it hurt the mongoose's ears. His stomach was full. He wanted to sleep some more, and for the life of him he could not understand why the birds were making such a terrible racket. Finally, he gave up trying to wait for all of them to fly away. He left the bush and returned to his former sleeping place under the leaves of the banyan tree. That is why to this very day, if you hear two birds of the Caribbean squabbling over one thing or another, it is almost certain that, sooner or later, one of them will screech at the other, "You have the heart of a mongoose!"

Some of you might be wondering what happened to the tiny hummingbird. She flew to the eave of the man's plantation house. There she built a nest, laid her eggs, and raised her young. And the man so loved to watch the colorful little bird flitting from flower to flower, gathering nectar in the morning, that he allowed no harm to come to her or her children from either snake or mongoose.

"The Heart of the Mongoose" and Real Life:

Today many people in the world no longer worship the one true God. Instead they worship science. They are the ones who tell you, "It is only a matter of time before science solves all of our problems on earth. All we have to do is trust our scientists." Anyone who really believes that is as foolish as the sugarbirds who trusted the mongoose. For, like the mongoose, science has no "heart." It is just as likely to create a terrible bomb that can turn a big city into ashes as it is to give mankind a pill that will cure disease.

Now, that does not mean there are no good men who are scientists. There are. The problem is that science itself is neither good nor evil; and it is foolish to worship something that cannot show you the difference between right and wrong. Sooner or later, that kind of a "god" is very likely to destroy you or your children.

People who try to separate God and science are like the sugarbirds who tried to separate the mongoose from his master, the man. In the end, they discovered to their great sorrow that the pit viper destroyed only one nest, whereas the mongoose destroyed them all.

Proverbs 14:12—"There is a way which seemeth right unto a man, but the end thereof are the ways of death."

The Legend of the Rats of Dunharrow

PART 1: DAMUS AND THE GREAT DIVISION

Once there were no rats in Dunharrow—or any other village of man, for that matter. They did not plunder barns for man's grain or steal bread from his cupboard or spread disease in his cities. They lived in the forest like other wild creatures and ate roots, berries, herbs, nuts, and seeds. But those days were long, long ago. All that remains of them is a legend the wood rats tell their children. It goes like this.

Once, all rats looked very much alike. They had long, bushy tails, tiny feet, big eyes and ears, and soft coats of fur. Still, there were three different families. The brown rats were the biggest and had brown hair. The black rats had black fur; and the wood rats could be brown or black, but their clan was the smallest in size and the fewest in number. They came by their curious name because they did not dig burrows deep in the earth like their cousins the brown and black rats. Instead, they built nests inside hollow trees, fallen logs, or beneath piles of underbrush.

95

But whatever clan a rat might be born into, he could still trace his family tree to one creature— Rathmus, the greatest rat who ever lived, and the wisest. The advice he gave to his sons and daughters passed by word of mouth from one generation of rats to another. Over the centuries, his sayings became so well known to the rats and to many other creatures of the forest that they were simply called "The Laws of Father Rathmus."

Now, one of those laws was "It is not for rats to taste man food. Nothing can come of it but death and sorrow." So, since the brown rats, black rats, and wood rats always obeyed Rathmus, they avoided men's houses. And for a long, long time that was not hard to do. The world was large, and men were few and scattered. Also, men lived and worked under the sun, whereas the rats searched for their food mostly by night.

But then one day, many men and women came together. They took axes and shovels and cleared a portion of the forest beside a wide river. They built cottages and barns. Around these, fields were plowed and planted with corn, wheat, and barley. As time passed, more people came. Soon shops were built for trade, and a big farmer's market, and a wooden wharf where fishermen could come and go with their boats and nets. Finally the men and women gave the place a name. They called it the Village of Dunharrow.

All of this caused a great stir among the forest animals. They were very curious about man and his village. But for the rats, the most interesting thing of all was its sewer.

The men who planned Dunharrow knew their village would keep growing. They wanted it always to be clean. So they made underground tunnels of stone and mortar, which led from the village to the river bank. Through this sewer, all of the village's garbage was carried to the river; and the river swept it away to the sea.

But the rats had no idea what a sewer was for. To them it was just a gigantic burrow of some kind, full of wonderful smells (for even in those days, human garbage was a tempting meal for a rat). And since the brown rats and black rats lived in tunnels in the ground and could see well in the dark, many was the time that one of their kind longed to crawl inside the sewer and explore. But they were afraid to draw too close to the world of man for fear of breaking the laws of Father Rathmus. So the rats kept away from Dunharrow and its sewer. At least, they did until Damus was born.

Damus was of the brown rat clan. There was nothing very unusual about him. He was not very large or strong or smart. And so, as he grew up with all of the other young brown rats, no one paid very much attention to him. And this made Damus terribly angry. He was not happy living his life like the other forest creatures. He longed to be important. And for Damus, to be really important meant only one thing—to someday become the king of the rat clans and have all of the other animals remember his sayings the way they remembered the words of Father Rathmus. But whenever he told his friends that, they would only laugh at him, because in those days the rat was one of the few animals in the forest who had no king. Damus spent most of his life trying to think of a way to become king of the rats. He thought night and day. And while he was thinking, he often watched the village of Dunharrow. He saw the men dig many new ditches for their stone and mortar sewer.

Damus's curiosity about men and their village deepened with each passing day. He knew that men had great power and that all other creatures feared them. So as Damus thought and watched, he also crept closer and closer to Dunharrow until one day he found himself sitting in front of the wide, round mouth of the sewer at the river's edge. He looked into the dark tunnel and muttered to himself, "If only I could go to the men's world and carry some of their power back to the forest with me. Then I could surely be the king of the rats."

For many hours Damus sat there watching and thinking. Finally a nightingale spotted him. The bird landed in a bush overhead and mournfully sang the words of Father Rathmus. "Nothing will come of it but death and sorrow." Damus looked up at the nightingale, grumbled to himself irritably, and slowly crawled back to his burrow in the forest.

But from that night on, Damus continued to return to the mouth of the sewer. Sometimes he would sit like a statue for hours staring into it and wondering what he would find if he stepped inside. But he was afraid of men; and even when he gathered enough courage to take a step toward the sewer, the warning of Father Rathmus rang in his ears and he stopped. If Damus had not entered the sewer of Dunharrow, rats today would probably be much the same as they were then. But late one night while Damus sat in front of the sewer's mouth watching and wondering, a red fox leaped down from the river bank and landed in the soft mud a few feet from him. The fox had only come to the river for a drink of water. He was not hunting for rats. So at first Damus went unnoticed, because he was sitting so very still. This gave Damus a chance to dash into the safety of the dark

sewer passage where the fox was afraid to follow.

Damus could have waited for the fox to leave and then returned to his burrow. But once he was inside the sewer, his curiosity about men overcame his fear of breaking Father Rathmus's laws. He scampered up the damp stone tunnel toward the village until he found himself beneath the streets of Dunharrow. There he discovered that the sewer had many smaller passages branching from the main one. In each there was food for a hundred rats. But Damus did not eat any of it even though he was very hungry. He was still afraid of man food.

But he continued to explore. At the end of one tunnel there was a hole just large enough for him to squeeze through. He looked and he listened, and when he was certain there was no danger, Damus crawled through the opening. He became the first rat to enter the world of man.

Damus found himself on a cold, stone floor inside one of man's shops. Although the brown rat did not know it, he was standing in the back room of the village butcher shop. All around, huge pieces of meat hung from hooks fastened to the rafters. He stood on his tiny back legs and sniffed the air. It was filled with the sweetest, most wonderful smells he had ever known. Damus noticed a scrap of beef laying on the floor beside the butcher's block. Ignoring the words of Father Rathmus, he hopped over and nibbled it. In that moment, Damus's life was forever changed. Suddenly, Damus's whole body craved the taste of man food. He scurried madly about the butcher shop hungrily searching for anything that smelled of man's meat. He gobbled up every scrap he could find. And when his little belly could hold no more, he saw the worlds of men and rats through different eyes. The sewer of Dunharrow was no longer frightening. The dark passages promised him just what he wanted, a place to rule as king of the rats. But first, he had to make the others follow him there.

Damus got an idea. He searched the floor of the butcher's shop until he found the biggest scrap of raw meat he could carry. He slung it across his shoulders and hurried back through the sewers to the river. There he washed it to get rid of the scent of man as best he could.

When Damus reached the forest, he tore the meat into small pieces. Then he ran from brown rat burrow to brown rat burrow burying them under the husks of chest nuts and scraps of bitter root that lay on the ground out side. Of course, rats have a keen sense of smell. So in no time at all, the rats crawled out of their burrows, and found the meat. Not knowing that it was man food, they ate it. Instantly, the rats changed. From that moment on, all they could think about was stuffing themselves with this wonderful new food. And they began to scamper madly about the forest floor searching for more.

When Damus saw how well his plan was working, he ran back to the butcher shop and stole more meat. He went to other burrows and repeated his trick. Before the night was over, every brown rat in the forest had tasted man food. And all of them were desperate to have more. Then Damus crawled on top of a great oak stump and shouted, "What is it you are looking for?"

"There is a new kind of food in the forest!" the brown rats cried back. "We have never tasted anything like it. It is so delicious that we must have more!"

"Oh, is that all?" Damus answered with a laugh. "I

know where there is so much of that food you couldn't eat it all in a lifetime!"

And the brown rats swarmed around the oak stump and begged Damus to show them where it was.

"Oh, no!" Damus replied. "There is something I must have first."

"Anything! Anything! Just show us where this wonderful food can be found," the brown rats shouted.

"Bring all of the other rats in the forest to my burrow tomorrow night; and then, I will lead you to the place where you can eat your fill of this new food."

The brown rats ran in every direction and alerted their cousins. The following night, the three clans gathered in a great crowd about the entrance to Damus's burrow. Everyone had heard of the strange, new food and wondered what Damus knew about it.

When Damus came up from his burrow, he had a piece of meat between his teeth. He tossed it into the crowd of brown rats. They battled one another for a bite of it. "Is that what you want?" asked Damus with a grin. "Well, there is no need to fight over it. I know a place where you can eat all that you can hold."

"Where? Where?" the brown rats squealed.

In the sewer of Dunharrow. And I can lead you through it. But first you must make me your king!"

As soon as the wood rats and black rats heard this, they cried with one voice. "You have broken the law of Father Rathmus! You must be punished!" But the big brown rats suddenly drew themselves into a circle around Damus. They cared for nothing now but getting more of the man food. They swore that they would rip in pieces the first rat who tried to lay a paw on Damus. This took the others by surprise. Never before had rat threatened to kill rat. The wild rats had always thought they had enough enemies in the forest without fighting among themselves.

A great argument began. One of the black rats cried, "Rats need no king!" And a wood rat squealed the words of Father Rathmus, "It is not for rats to taste man food! Nothing can come of it but death and sorrow!"

But Damus replied, "I have eaten man food for two days, and I am not dead, and I've never been so full and happy. Besides, all of our enemies in the forest are afraid of men. If we lived in the sewer of Dunharrow, we would be safe from harm. None of them would dare to follow us there."

Now, when the black rats heard this and saw that all of their bigger cousins were ready to do what Damus asked, they decided to join them. For like the brown rats, they lived in holes deep in the earth, and the sewer of Dunharrow seemed to them like a giant burrow. But the little wood rats did not want to be underground. They loved the smell of trees around them. So one after the other, they left Damus's burrow for their own homes in the forest.

And that is how the great division of the rats took place. The wood rats remained in the wild. But the black rats and brown rats made Damus their king, and he led them into the sewer of Dunharrow where they ate man food for the rest of their lives. And so did their children and grandchildren and great-great-great grandchildren.

Of course, life in the dark sewer changed the black rats and brown rats. Their fur grew dark, oily, and filthy from eating the garbage tossed into the sewer. They lost all of the hair on their once-bushy tails. Their bodies grew long and narrow because they were always having to squeeze through tight places. They learned how to sneak out of the sewer at night and plunder men's cupboards and storehouses, and the filth they carried in their fur began making people sick.

The worst thing about the brown and black rats was how wasteful they became. They grew lazy, fat, and careless. They spoiled more food than they ate. It was not that they hated man or wanted to harm him by destroying so much of his property; they simply did not care about anything but themselves.

The more the rats lived in man's world, the more their habits changed to suit it. They began hiding inside wagons and freight. So the people of Dunharrow, without knowing it, began carrying whole families of rats to other places where villages were being built. In this way the brown and black rat clans spread across the land.

As King Damus had promised, the rats were safe from their enemies in the sewer. Their numbers grew and grew. One day, after a hundred generations of rats had lived and died beneath the streets of Dunharrow, the dark passages could not hold all of them. Bitter fighting broke out between the two clans. Finally, the bigger brown rats drove out the black rats.

But the black rats did not return to the forest. They had eaten man food much too long. It was all that they wanted now. But since they were afraid of the larger brown rats, they kept away from cellars where they might happen to meet one. The black rats learned to build homes above ground among attic rafters, barn lofts, or inside house walls. Many left Dunharrow to live on farms near the village. There they destroyed haystacks and corn cribs.

And that was how rats came to look and act like

they do today. But that is not the end of the story. One day, the men of Dunharrow grew angry at the rats for the terrible things they were doing. They decided to stop them. And that is the second part of the legend of the rats of Dunharrow.

The Legend of the Rats of Dunharrow

PART 2: SUDARATHMUS AND THE WAY OF ESCAPE

Years passed. The village of Dunharrow grew into a very large town. The brown and black rats who lived in its sewers and attics forgot how life had once been in the land. Most had no idea who Father Rathmus was, much less what he had said. They only remembered the advice left by old King Damus. And he had taught them how to break into men's storehouses or steal food from their cupboards.

Even the little wood rats changed in time. Although they still called Rathmus "Father," they no longer followed his laws so closely. The truth was that many of their clan also wandered into man's fields and ate his crops just like their bigger cousins. But the wood rats never left the forest. They had no king, and they still looked very much like the rats of Damus's age.

It was into this new day of rats and men that a young wood rat called Suds was born. His parents actually named him Sudarathmus. But the other wood rats had a difficult time remembering that. So they shortened his name to Suds.

In a way, Suds was a little like Damus. The older he got, the more curious he became about men. He spent a lot of his time studying them. But he was not at all like old Damus in another way. Suds never wanted to be important. He did not like the attention the other rats in the forest gave him. And they paid a lot of attention to him, because Suds had the oddest habit any of them had seen. The little wood rat traded with men.

Often, he could be seen at night scampering toward a farmhouse or creeping close to some shepherd who was sleeping beneath the stars. Then, if he found anything shiny or colorful and small enough for him to carry—a ring, a coin, a button, or a spoon—he would take it back to his home in the forest. And in its place, he would leave something that was of great value to a wood rat, like an acorn or a tasty seed. Suds lined his nest with "treasures" from man's world. And this caused the wood rats to give him another nickname. They called him "the little merchant."

Well, it happened that one night, as Suds was wandering along the edge of a dirt path that led to Dunharrow, he spied a man sleeping beneath a tall elm tree. Suds crept up to him. A leather pouch lay on the ground beside the sleeping man. When Suds peeked inside it, his eyes grew wide with surprise. There was the largest gold ring he had ever seen in his life.

The little merchant scurried into the nearby woods. He knew just where there was a tall chestnut tree with beautiful, big chestnuts. Suds found ten of the best. One by one, he brought them to the sleeping man. "There," he whispered to himself. "A fair trade if ever I saw one." And he reached inside the leather pouch, grabbed the big golden ring, and carried it home.

Suds lived inside a huge, fallen oak log. Like all wood rats, he had a great nest fashioned from grass and sticks and tree bark. It had many tunnels that led in and out of holes in the old oak's trunk. At the middle of this nest he

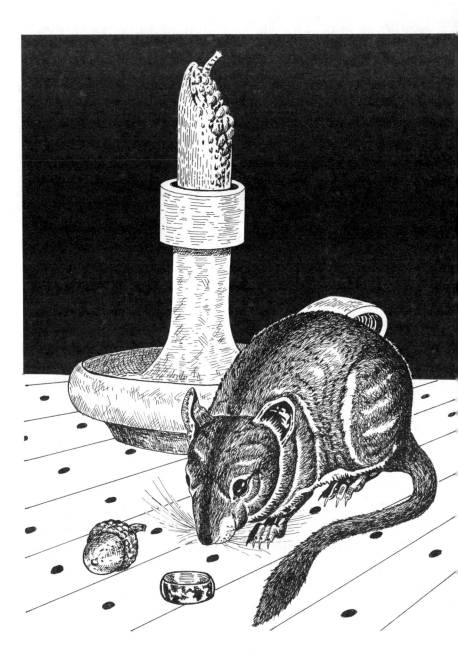

had hollowed out a wide room where he slept with his treasures gathered around him.

He placed the ring among the rest of his collection and sat down to admire it. That is when he noticed something very strange. One side of the ring was wide, thick, and flat. On this part, the head of a rat had been carved into the shiny metal. Suds eyed the ring and wondered at the carving for a long time. But finally he grew very sleepy and curled up with the golden ring clutched in his paws. And Suds had a terrible dream.

He dreamed that he was some place deep under the earth. It was so dark that the only way to find a path was to feel with his whiskers and paws. Suds knew he must be in a cave of some kind because there were rocks beneath his feet, and all around he heard the noise of water dripping into shallow pools.

Then, a strange smell filled Suds' nose. Smoke! It stung his eyes and made him sneeze.

Suddenly another sound reached his keen ears. In the distance he heard squealing, and when he realized what made the noise, he began to tremble with fear. He was listening to a thousand rat voices screaming for help as they searched frantically for a way to escape some awful trap.

The smell of smoke grew stronger. Suds gasped for air! He knew that he must escape the darkness. His instincts told him that the light was far above him. So, he felt the hard stone floor with his tiny feet and his long whiskers, and wherever the stones led upward he followed them. He scurried up and up as fast as his little legs would carry him. Finally, he saw sunlight. It poured through a tiny hole leading from the terrible darkness to safety. Suds dashed through it! Instantly, the smoke and the dripping water and squealing rats vanished.

Suds blinked his eyes against the harsh light. He was sitting on a tree limb. At his back was a hole that led into his oak tree home. The awful dream had been so real that it caused him to run in his sleep through one of the tunnels of his nest.

Suds looked around in confusion. It was a bright, hot summer day. A large black and gold butterfly flitted past his head. Above, the sky was soft blue without so much as the wisp of a cloud. Suds raised a shaky paw. He licked it and began to wash his long whiskers. He mumbled to himself, "What on earth was that all about? Oh, Father Rathmus, I think that was the worst dream I've had in my entire life!"

Suds returned to his nest. He looked at the golden ring with the head of the rat carved into it. And the more he studied it, the more he thought about his dream. Suddenly Suds wished he had kept the ten chestnuts and left the man's ring in the leather pouch. Even though it was early in the afternoon and all other wood rats were still fast asleep, Suds decided to leave his home and search for food.

He remembered an apple tree atop a high hill that overlooked Dunharrow. And it was that time of year when he thought the limbs should be full of ripe apples. If the wind had knocked some to the ground, they would make a tasty meal. So he climbed out of his home in the oak tree and scampered through the forest. The path to the apple tree took Suds to the edge of a wide cornfield. Beyond that field was the hill where the tree grew. And on the far side of the hill was Dunharrow.

Suds knew the farmer who planted the cornfield. The little merchant had traded with the man several times.

Suds left some fine plump acorns at his farmhouse in exchange for buttons or brass coins.

Suds hurried across the field, expecting to find row after row of corn, tall and green with large, tassled ears thrusting out in every direction. But when Suds ran a short distance into the field, he stopped short. Hundreds of cornstalks lay on the ground rotting in the sun.

Suds shook his head in wonder. He sniffed one of the broken stumps and instantly knew what had happened.

"Black rats!" Suds whispered. The stalks had been cut in two by the sharp teeth of a member of their clan. Then, when the corn fell to the ground, the rest of the black rats had swarmed over the ears and stripped them to their red cobs. Suds knew this black rat trick well, but never had he seen so much destruction in one place.

On the far side of the wrecked field was a deep ditch that wound along the foot of the hill where the apple tree stood. The farmer had dug it to catch rainwater that ran down the slope. When Suds reached the ditch and started to cross, he heard a loud crunching sound, like the snapping of dry brush under the feet of a large animal. At first, he thought it might be an enemy and hopped under the cover of some broken cornstalks. But when he sniffed the air, he just smelled more rats.

Suds crept into the ditch. He moved slowly and ever so quietly in the direction of the noise, ready at any moment to dash for safety. He rounded a turn in the ditch and there sat two large black rats with what was left of a chicken, gnawing loudly on the bones. Suds saw the blood on their whiskers and squeaked with horror. The two black rats whirled in surprise.

"You—you've k-killed one of the farmer's hens!'

Suds stammered, seeing the cold gleam in the black rats' eyes.

One of the black rats grumbled angrily at him, "Go on, ya stinkin' wood rat! Go kill yer own. There ain't enough here fer the two o' us."

"Father Rathmus!" Suds cried. "How could you do such a terrible thing? Rats were never meant to kill other animals."

And suddenly, the two black rats began to laugh very loud. One looked at the other and asked, "Wot do you make o' that there, mate?"

"It's 'ard to say. Maybe it comes from breathin' too much 'o that there bloomin' fresh air," chuckled the second.

Suds snapped, "First you black rats destroy the farmer's field and now you kill his chickens. Do you think he will let you go on acting like this forever? Sooner or later he is sure to punish you for these terrible crimes!"

Suddenly the two black rats stopped laughing and again stared angrily at Suds. "Ain't that jus' like a bloomin' wood rat," grumbled the first. "Always in a mind that they're better'n the rest o' us poor workin' chaps."

The second black rat snarled at Suds, " 'Fore ya get to lookin' too far down yer silly nose at us black rats, ya'd better take a look at them there brown rats!"

"Right ya are, mate. Right ya are!" chimed the first. "Ya don't see one o' our clan gobblin' up another rat!" And he shook with disgust. "Ain't nothin' in this 'ere world worse'n a brown rat!"

"That there's the truth, mate!" said the other as he scratched through the pile of feathers looking for another bone. "That there is the blinkin' truth. Why jus' the other day I heard that one o' their bunch bit a man-child. They say the little chap took sick and died."

Again the first black rat shuddered, "Filthy beasts, them there brown rats," he spat. "No black rat'd go 'round bitin' a man-child—not if 'e didn't try to grab one o' us er nuthin'!"

"I tell ya, mate, it does me soul good jus' to know that none o' me kin could ever be bad as a brown rat!" the second rat snorted, and the two of them ignored little Suds from that moment on and again began to gnaw loudly on the chicken bones. The sight and sound of the two black rats caused Suds to feel sick to his stomach. He scurried out of the ditch and up the hill to get away from them.

When he reached the apple tree, he found dozens of fine, red apples lying on the ground. But he had lost his appetite. So he climbed a tall rock to watch the village of Dunharrow stretched out below the hill.

Suds wondered at what he saw there. It looked as though every man, woman, and child in the village was standing in the streets. They carried shovels, long sticks, and large boxes. All of them were listening to one man, who stood on a barrel in the center of town. He pointed this way and that and spoke loudly in the man tongue. And whichever direction he pointed, groups of people went carrying their shovels, sticks, and boxes. Suds stood on his hind legs and stared curiously at the man on the barrel. He could not be sure because the man was so far away, but he thought it was the same one with whom he had traded during the night. Finally Suds mumbled to himself, "Well, I guess there is no point in sitting here all afternoon. I'll go home and try to sleep." But when Suds hopped to the earth from the top of the tall rock, he tumbled through the thick grass into a deep hole.

Quickly, Suds scurried out of the hole and then turned to stare into its dark mouth. It lay hidden from view under the tall rock. It was no animal den, or, if it ever had been, nothing had lived there for a long time. Suds sniffed deeply. The air smelled damp and stale. His nose sensed passages far under the earth. He did not know how or why, but something deep in his heart told him this hole led to the place in his awful dream.

Suds trembled with fear. He wanted to run away from this spot and never return to it; but he remembered the voices of the rats squealing for help. If there was anything he could do to save them he must at least try. Slowly, he crept into the dark opening.

It led down and down. The way was so steep that he had a hard time not falling head first into the deep tunnel. Finally the narrow passage opened into a wide cave. Suds heard the steady drip of water as it fell into shallow pools, just as he had heard that sound in his dream.

Now, wood rats have a keen sense of direction, and they certainly are not afraid of the dark since they spend most of their lives hunting for food at night. Suds knew the way back to the apple tree, and he also knew that he was growing close to the village of Dunharrow with each step he took. The hole in the hill was in fact a large crack between great boulders. This crack fell into deep limestone caves that fanned out in many directions. But always the caves led farther and farther into the earth. Most would have been far too small for a man to squeeze into; but for a tiny wood rat they were like giant caverns.

As Suds felt his way through the pitch-black caves, he came to many stone walls and had to retrace his steps, then start again. But dead ends were not the real problem. What worried Suds was that he really did not know where he was trying to go. All he knew was that in his dream he had heard the voices of many rats crying for help. But where they were in this dark maze, Suds had no idea. The longer he stayed in the caves, the more discouraged he became. Suds was ready to give up the search and turn back. Then he sneezed. And a rat's voice suddenly exclaimed, "What was that?"

"What was what?" another rat asked. "I didn't hear anything."

The sound of the voices led Suds to a small crack in the rocks. He could see the tiniest bit of light coming from the other side, and he smelled a terrible odor.

"I guess I'm just nervous about what the men are doing, the first voice said a moment later.

"So they're blocking a few holes into the sewer. What of it? King Damus showed us how to make others. Besides, men can't touch us here.

"Don't be too sure," answered the first voice. "The men are very powerful; and I think they hate us now ever since the man-child died."

"What's gotten into you lately, Macro?" the other voice asked. "Are you going soft? You'd better watch your step. If the king ever hears talk like that you'll wind up as dinner for the clan!"

"All right. But we'd better report what we've seen. We could be eaten for not doing that, too!"

Suds saw two large shadows slip past the crack in the stones. He knew from the sound of their voices they were brown rats, which meant he had found a secret way to the sewer of Dunharrow from the top of the hill.

For the longest time he just sat by the small crack in the wall of the sewer and thought. The two black rats had spoken the truth. Long years in the sewer of Dunharrow had changed the brown rats into cannibals, and now they were responsible for a man-child's death.

"How terrible!" Suds whispered to himself. "Why, even if they needed rescuing, I wouldn't want to do it."

He decided to go back to the apple tree. Suds climbed up and up. He remembered the way back and never made a single wrong turn, but the climb was steep and hard. He often had to stop and rest. By the time he crawled out of the hole under the tall rock, it was late in the afternoon.

Suds blinked at the bright light, and when he could see again he noticed right away that the sky looked very different than it had earlier that day. No longer was it clear and blue. The air was full of black clouds. But they were not like any storm clouds he had ever seen.

Suddenly there was a rustle in the grass. Out hopped a black rat, his eyes wild with fear.

"What happened to you?"exclaimed Suds.

The black rat squealed in terror and started to run away. But Suds shouted for him to wait. When the black rat saw that it was only a tiny wood rat, he fell down in the dust, panting and groaning. Then, he began to repeat over and over again, "The men—the men—the men—"

"What about the men?" Suds asked fearfully.

"Can't ya see them there clouds o' smoke?" whimpered the black rat. "The men came for us with torches. They set fire to fields an' 'ay stacks where we was sleepin'. They sent ferrets into our nests in the barns and corn cribs. Them 'orrible little weasels chased us out where men was waitin' with sticks an' shovels. They killed us by the hundreds. Not even the young was spared!" Then the black rat sobbed loudly, "It was 'orrible

117

to see. Nothin' like that should even 'appen to a brown rat!"

"Father Rathmus!' Suds exclaimed. "But it *will* happen to them if I don't do something!" Now he saw everything clearly. Now he knew what his dream had meant. The day of judgment had arrived for the rats of Dunharrow. The men were punishing them for all the crimes they had committed since Damus and the great division.

"Do you believe that all rats were brothers once?" he asked the terrified black rat. The black rat nodded. "Then however evil the brown rats may be, they are still our kin. And you must help me save them, because what happened to the black rats today will happen to the brown rats tomorrow!"

The black rat thought about this for a little while, and finally he agreed to help.

"Then follow me!" cried Suds, and he darted into the hole under the tall rock with the black rat at his heels.

Their journey through the caves was slower than Suds had hoped. The black rat did not know the way, and his clan had lived above ground for so long that he was afraid of dark places in the earth. Suds had to coax him every step of the way. By the time they reached the crack in the sewer wall, Suds knew it must be late in the night.

"I don't know a thing about digging," said Suds. "Can you open this hole so we can get through?'

"I'll do me best, mate!" answered the black rat and he began to dig and bite at the crumbling mortar of the sewer wall. In no time at all, a stone broke loose. Suds and the black rat pushed with all their might, and the stone fell with a loud clatter into the sewer passage. Suds hopped through the hole and landed on cold, wet stones. For as far as he could see in both directions, the long, round tunnel was empty.

The black rat poked his head through the hole and whispered nervously, "Where is this 'ere place?"

"It's the sewer of Dunharrow."

The black rat began to tremble. "They's brown rats in 'ere," he mumbled.

"Of course there are brown rats in here," Suds squeaked. "We've come to save them. They are our brothers."

The black rat looked first one direction and then the other. Finally, he whimpered, "Supposin' these 'ere brown rats don't feel very brotherly toward us?"

Suds could see that the black rat was terrified. And even though he thought that he might need his help again, he said, "All right, you've been through enough today. Wait here, black rat. I'll go and find them by myself."

Suds turned and scampered up the sewer passage in the direction he had seen the brown rats go earlier.

The sewer was as big a maze as the caves and almost as dark. But Suds did not have to travel very far before he ran into a pair of brown rats. As soon as they saw Suds, they came at him with their long fangs bared. But they stopped when the little wood rat cried, "I have a message for your king! The brown rat clan is in great danger!"

The two rats stopped and looked at one another. Finally, one of them motioned for the little wood rat to follow. He scurried up a small tunnel. Suds was right behind him. And behind Suds was the other brown rat.

The small tunnel led to a bigger one, and the bigger

tunnel came to an end at a great round chamber. Many passages led in and out of this chamber, and it was full of rotting garbage and brown rats. There, sleeping on a broken wood box in the middle of the round chamber, was the biggest, fattest rat Suds had ever seen in his life.

All the brown rats grew very quiet when they saw Suds. This caused the huge rat to wake up. When he spotted the little wood rat, his eyes grew wide with surprise.

"Where did he come from?" the huge rat growled.

"I don't know, sir," replied the rat who had led Suds to this place. "He just came up to us and said he had a message for you. He said the clan was in danger."

The king of the brown rats stretched himself from head to toe and yawned. He stood up and cried with a loud voice, "Let the trial begin!" And rats began to pour into the round chamber from the surrounding pipes. They crowded around Suds and pushed him closer and closer to the huge rat. Finally, the floor of the chamber was a solid mass of rats except for that small space in the center where Suds, the box, and the king of the brown rats stood.

"Trial?" Suds asked the king. "What trial?"

The king of the brown rats replied, "Why, your trial, of course. The law is clear. Only brown rats are allowed in the sewer of Dunharrow. All others must be killed and eaten! But I am a fair king. I am always willing to hear a criminal's defense, no matter how tasty—I mean, guilty—he might be." Suds was terrified. He knew by the look of the vicious king that there was no way to reason with him. So he turned to the crowd of brown rats and cried. "Today, the men destroyed the black rat clan. Only a few escaped with their lives!"

120

"Good!" snorted the king of the brown rats. "It serves their filthy kind right!" And there was a rumble of agreement from the other brown rats.

Suds said, "The men killed them because of the terrible things they did. Black rats wasted fields and robbed storehouses and killed farm animals. But brown rats have done all this and something much worse. A brown rat caused the death of a man-child. So, tomorrow, what happened to the black rats will happen to you."

"Nonsense!" hissed the king of the brown rats.

"How can men touch us here? We are safe in the sewer, as the wise king Damus promised we would be!"

Suds turned quickly and spat, "If you want to know how, I can tell you. They have sealed most of the holes leading in and out of the sewer. They are going to fill this place with smoke, and you will either smother or run outside to face the men who will be waiting to crush you with their weapons!" Deep fear swept over the crowd of rats. All of them knew that the men were closing many of their tunnels.

Suds saw this and cried hopefully, "But I have found a way of escape! It is not very far from here, and I can lead you through it to safety in the forest!"

The brown rats grew very quiet and waited for their king's command. The huge rat solemnly answered, "You have always called me a fair king. Well, our sewer is very large. I would never be able to spread this news to all of our brothers and sisters by tomorrow. Would I be a fair king if I allowed some brown rats to go with this wood rat while others were left behind to suffer, and all because they didn't know about this way of escape?"

Suds whirled and screeched in the rat king's face, "Are you crazy? They aren't going to die just because they don't know of the way of escape! They are going to die because the brown rats chose to live in this terrible sewer in the first place! The rats who know how to escape should do it!"

The big rat began to tremble with rage. There was murder in his eyes. "No one talks to a king of the brown rats like that!" he squealed. "The men are no danger to us. And the only rat in this sewer who is going to do any dying is you, wood rat!" And he coiled like a snake and prepared to jump on little Suds.

Suds closed his eyes. There was nowhere for him to run. He knew that he was lost. But at that instant, a high pitched scream echoed from one of the dark sewer tunnels. "Fire in the sewer! The men are upon us! Run for your lives!"

The brown rats were so nervous about what Suds had told them that they panicked when they heard the cry. Suds was trampled under the feet of an army of terrified, squealing rats. When he opened his eyes again, he was all alone beside the broken woodbox, and he was covered from head to toe with filth from the chamber floor. The brown rats had fled into the maze of tunnels.

He looked all around the big empty room. Suddenly, he saw the face of the black rat peek cautiously from around a corner. The black rat smiled and said, "I changed me mind and decided to tag along after all."

"Then you gave the alarm!" Suds squeaked happily. "That there is just what I did, mate. But I don't think it'll fool them brown rats for long. So we ought to be goin' back the way we came."

Suds looked around sadly. "I guess you're right. They didn't believe me. And now the brown rat clan is doomed." He turned and started to scurry away when a voice called, "Wait for us!" And a whole family of brown rats appeared from the darkness of a nearby passage. The black rat's fur bristled. But Suds told him to be still.

The father of the brown rat family came up to them and said, "My name is Macro, and I want you to lead my family to safety!"

"Macro!" Suds squeaked. "You were the rat on the other side of the sewer wall today when I sneezed."

The brown rat stared at him with surprise. "So you made that noise!"

"Yes, and your voice led me to the sewer! Do you remember the spot?" Macro nodded. "Well, that is where the way of escape can be found. If I stay in the sewer, the king of the brown rats will have me killed. But you can go anywhere you like. Run and tell your clan about the way of escape. The black rat and I will wait for you there with your family. Then, we will lead as many brown rats as we can to safety." Macro turned instantly and dashed into another tunnel. Suds, the black rat, and Macro's family made their way through the sewer to the hole in its wall. Then they crawled into the caves and waited.

In a little while, Suds heard the scratching of rat claws on the stone floor of the sewer. He stuck his head out of the hole and saw a mother rat coming followed by six children. More appeared—male and female, young and old. And Suds squeaked to them to climb into the hole that led out of the sewer. Suds did not count how many rats joined him in the caves, but he knew it was only the smallest fraction of the brown rat clan.

Hours passed. Suds knew that the time was growing short because he felt the ground above him tremble with the footsteps of many men. He wished with all his heart that Macro would show up. Then his nose smelled a bitter odor much different from the awful stink of the sewer. Smoke! The men's deadly work had begun.

He turned quickly and called to the black rat, "You know the way back, don't you?"

"I do, mate!" called the black rat from far away in the caves.

"Then take these rats to safety. I am going to wait here for Macro."

So the other rats left and Suds stood halfway in the sewer and halfway out of it waiting and watching. Slowly, the tunnel began to fill with smoke. It burned his eyes and nose. Soon, he could see no more than a few feet in any direction. He began to choke. But Suds refused to leave.

"Oh, Macro," the little wood rat squealed in fear, "Please come on. You've saved so many tonight, can't you save yourself?"

And just then a voice in the distance cried, "Is that you, wood rat? I'm lost in this smoke!"

It was Macro! Suds squealed with joy. He shouted and shouted as loud as he could. Macro followed his voice to the hole in the wall and crawled inside the cave. And the two of them began to climb up and up toward the apple tree on top of the hill. The little wood rat stopped only once when he heard a terrible echo in the caves. His blood ran cold. Hundreds of brown rats were running through the sewer squealing in terror. But in the thick smoke they could not find the way of escape. His awful dream had come true.

When Suds and Macro reached the tall rock and crawled outside, the little wood rat counted only a hundred rats who had been saved from the sewer of

124

Dunharrow. He hung his head in sorrow and said, "Father Rathmus was right. All that came of it was death and sorrow. Sorrow for the men. Death for the rats."

Suds led the troop of rats down the hill and into the forest. It took a long time, but finally he found places in the woods for each of them to hide and rest. Then Suds took Macro and his family and the black rat to his home in the fallen oak tree, and they all fell fast asleep.

Suds awoke before any of the others. It was night. He grabbed the big golden ring and carried it through the forest and across the burned cornfield to the farmer's house. Suds left it sitting on the man's table and took nothing in return. He just wanted to be rid of that terrible ring and all of its memories.

The next morning the farmer was shocked to see the ring on his table, and he was also very pleased. You see, in those days, men had kings too. And the king of that land had offered a reward to anyone who could find the lost ring, which was the seal of his royal rat-catcher.

So the rats of Dunharrow were destroyed. But by this time, the black and brown rat clans had spread so far across the land that the men could not manage to wipe out all of them. It is their offspring who trouble us today. But the hundred rats who followed Suds into the way of escape never again returned to the world of man. As time passed, their children and grandchildren began to look like rats of the old age before the great division.

Of course, Suds became a great hero because he risked his life for the rats of Dunharrow. And that is why, to this very day, wood rats (or pack rats as they are sometimes called) trade with men. They do it to honor the memory of Sudarathmus, the little merchant.

"The Legend of the Rats of Dunharrow" and Real Life:

The Bible tells us about a man named Adam. Like Damus the brown rat, he broke a law—one that God made for men. And when he did that, he led all of his children, including you and me, down a dark path we never should have traveled.

Men changed after Adam's sin in the Garden of Eden, just like the brown and black rats changed when they lived in the sewer of Dunharrow. They became greedy and destructive. They began to hate their brothers. They learned how to steal and how to kill. They became everything God never wanted them to be. They changed so much that after a while God had to say about men, "Thou lovest evil more than good; and lying rather than to speak righteousness.(Psalm 52:3) ."

The rats of Dunharrow thought they were safe in the sewer, no matter how many terrible things they did. But they were wrong. The men punished them. And God says that He must one day punish men for their crimes. The Bible tells us that the penalty for man's sin is death. But the rats in the sewer had a way of escape, and so do we—Jesus, the Savior. The Bible says, "For God sent not His Son into the world to condemn the world; but that the world through Him might be saved (John 3:17)." And God commands Christians to do just what Suds and Macro did for the rats of Dunharrow: to go and lead others to the way of escape.

But often, people give the silliest excuse you could ever imagine for not accepting Christ's offer of safety. They say, "There is a man living somewhere in the world who never heard about Jesus. It is just not fair for us to take the way of escape and leave that poor fellow behind.

126

The answer to this, of course, is what Suds told the brown rat king. That man will not be punished because he hasn't heard about the way of escape. He will be punished because he and his fathers, all the way back to Adam himself, chose to live in an earthly "sewer" full of every imaginable evil in the first place.

Romans 5:12—"For God sent not His Son into the world to condemn the world; but that the world through Him might be saved."

John 14:6— "Jesus saith unto him, I am the way, the truth, and the life: no man cometh unto the Father, but by me."